Annihilation:

A Story of the Armenian Genocide

Michael Bosland

 Publishing

Annihilation: A Story of the Armenian Genocide
Published by Read All Over Publishing

www.michaelbosland.com
ISBN 978-1-7341662-1-7
Cover photos by iStock
Author photo by M. King
Book Cover Design by Chilton Creative

To those who were massacred during the genocides of World War I. To those who survived despite being forced to endure unspeakable horrors. And to the descendants who keep their memories alive.

Content

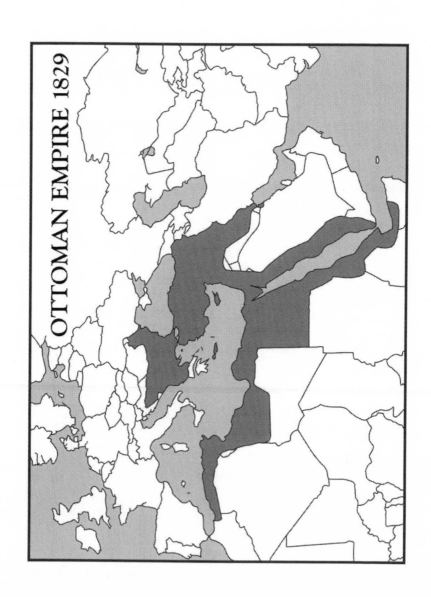

OTTOMAN EMPIRE 1829

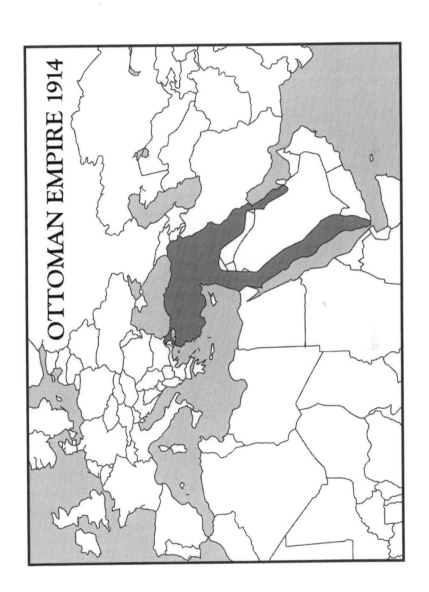

OTTOMAN EMPIRE 1914

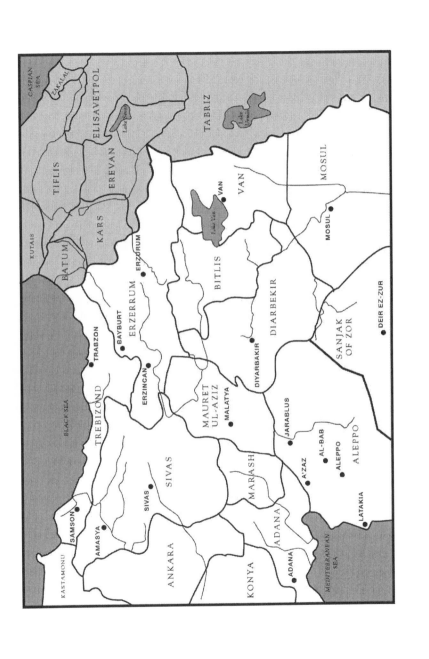

Epigraph

22 August 1939

"Our strength is our speed and our brutality...I have provided my Death-Head Units with orders to mercilessly and without compassion, send men, women, and children...to their death... Who still speaks today of the annihilation of the Armenians?"

Adolf Hitler

Kaj Mohmod

Bedros Elmassian strolled down Bayburt's main street after picking up the gold coins for the monthly payment to the prince. He tried to look as casual as he could—just another leisurely walk home for a quiet evening with his family. He turned down the narrow dirt alley that connected the main street to the only paved road in town. Two blocks down Emerald Street, past the giant houses of the Bayburt elite, and Bedros would reach his comfortable home at the edge of town. The prince's men would collect the family's tribute in the morning.

Kaj Mohmod saw Bedros and his heart began to race. He slipped quietly into the alley and stepped into the entrance of a small courtyard. Time seemed to stand still as Kaj held his breath, waiting. *It's taking too long. He should be here by now.* The waiting…always the waiting. *Really, he should be here by now.*

Then the march of time reasserted itself, marked by the sound of Bedros' footsteps as he moved through the alley. Kaj stiffened and gripped the handle of his hatchet so tightly that he could feel his hand going numb. As he listened to every step getting closer and closer, an intense tingling raced throughout his body. He had to move, to jump, to stomp, to shuffle… anything.

Finally, Bedros passed by. Kaj crept into the alley behind him. He raised his hatchet high above his head, then drove it down as hard as he could. In his excitement, Kaj had lunged too far forward. Instead of splitting his target's head with the blade, the handle of his weapon crashed down on Bedros's shoulder.

Bedros recoiled in pain but recovered his legs without falling. He straightened up and turned to face his attacker.

Kaj screamed in frustration, swinging his hatchet like an Olympic hammer thrower. This time the blade found its mark, splitting Bedros's face above the lower jaw. Bedros collapsed in agony, his blood spraying all over Kaj. The hatchet blade snapped out of Bedros's head. Still screaming, Kaj dropped to his knees and continued to pound the hatchet into the shattered skull over and over until the blade stuck. Then he rolled the body over and reached into the pocket of Bedros's jacket.

It's not here. It has to be here. Working for the infidels at the town's only bank was humiliating. Kaj was from a successful family that owned a spice business in Tsarevo. They lost the business, and everything else, in 1912 when the Bulgarian army chased them from their homes. In the mad rush to reach the safety of Constantinople, Kaj was separated from his family.

He arrived in the capital of the Ottoman Empire alongside thousands of other nameless refugees. Finding only rejection, he started a long, lonely trek east looking for work. When he arrived in Bayburt, his business experience helped him land a job at the bank. He hated it. The pay was horrible—barely enough to live on. Worse yet, the bank was managed by an

Armenian man. Seeing an inferior race living better than his own people distressed Kaj at the nucleus of his soul. His rage was unbearable.

But the degrading position had its perks. On the first day of every month, Kaj observed Bedros Elmassian withdraw from the bank one gold coin for everyone in his extended Armenian family. The money was in a small leather purse, which Bedros placed into the left inside pocket of his coat.

Kaj punched Bedros's dead body in the chest and screamed. He checked again. *It has to be here.* But no, the pocket was empty. Kaj flailed away like a child having a temper tantrum until his right hand was jolted by a shock of sudden pain. He had hit something hard on Bedros's right side. No, it was his left side. In his enraged state, Kaj had checked the wrong pocket.

"Hey, what are you doing there?"

Kaj jumped to his feet. He tried to run but tripped over the bloody mass that had been Bedros. Covered in blood and holding the sack of gold, Kaj was caught.

The Bedrosians

The day was winding down and most of the chores were done. Rosmerta was helping Shushawn clean up after dinner. Usually, she hated the task, but after such a fantastic day Rosmerta didn't mind.

Shushawn married Rosmerta's eldest brother Aghavni five years ago when Rosmerta was eight. Since Rosmerta's own mother had died giving birth to her, Shushawn was the closest thing to a mother she ever had. Shushawn and Aghavni had two children of their own. Anaguel was three and Megerdich, named after Rosmerta's father, was almost a year old.

Between Aghavni and Rosmerta, Megerdich had two other sons. Hagop was married to Adelina who was eight months pregnant. The youngest son, Papken, was getting most of the attention lately.

But Rosmerta didn't mind because, today, Shushawn had let Rosmerta make the yogurt by herself. Rosmerta had been making yogurt for years but this was the first time Shushawn was not watching her every move. Shushawn often said that *tanabour* was the most important part of any meal, and you can't make good tanabour without good yogurt. Rosmerta was pretty sure that bread must be more important than tanabour—all meals involved bread. Still, she appreciated that Shushawn was trying to make her feel good about her contribution. Rosmerta insisted that she knew how to make yogurt. Shushawn always agreed and promised to let her do it by herself next time. But when the next time came, she had always been watching.

But today Shushawn had left the house, leaving the yogurt to Rosmerta. When Rosmerta saw her leave, she was sure she would be right back. When foam formed on the goat milk, she glanced up to check the door—there was no one there. She removed the milk from the fire and checked the door again—still nothing. Shushawn was really gone! This time it was wholly up to Rosmerta. She rocked back and forth, shifting her weight between her legs as her excitement turned to nervousness. What if she made a mistake? But by the time she added the starter yogurt, Rosmerta knew it was going to work. She had done everything perfectly. Her legs steadied and she raised her head like a sunflower reaching for the morning light. Now she wished Shushawn had been there to see what a great job she had done.

When Shushawn returned, she simply stated that as soon as the yogurt was ready, she would show Rosmerta how to make tanabour. Rosmerta couldn't wait.

For now, the milk was fermenting and the dishes were clean. It was time to relax with the family. Rosmerta and Shushawn returned to the center of their simple, yet comfortable, house. The brown mud that was prevalent in the region was used to make a brick wall that surrounded a small courtyard containing two peach trees. A doorway led to a small room with a dirt floor. A partition divided the room in half. On one side lived three sheep, one mule, and a goat. Megerdich Bedrosian lived with his extended family on the other side.

As the patriarch of the family, Megerdich would normally organize the family's social and business relations in town. But he was getting old, and many of those responsibilities had fallen to Aghavni. Aghavni's wife, Shushawn kept things on track in the Bedrosian household.

The women joined the others gathered around the *tonir* in the middle of the living quarters. The tonir was the center of life in the house. The circular covered fire pit was the heat source during the winter, the oven, the stove, and the table for eating meals. This late at night, there were only a few nuts on it for munching. The family sat in a circle around the fire with their feet tucked under a blanket stretched over the tonir.

"Put the cards away," said Shushawn as she found a spot on the floor. She looked at Papken who was sitting quietly between his brothers.

"One more game," begged Hagop. "We're tied and we have to play again to determine a winner."

"Okay, but just one more."

Hagop dealt four cards face down to Aghavni, four to himself, and four face up, in the middle of the tonir.

"Two jacks: deal again," said Aghavni.

Hagop grunted and swept the cards up to try again.

"Come on, *Anagueljan*, you can help me."

Anaguel smiled at her father, the term of endearment lifting her heart.

"You win all the time—why do you get help?" Hagop complained.

Aghavni shrugged. "Because Anaguel and I are a team," he said, smiling back at his daughter.

"Okay, then I get Rosmerta."

Rosmerta slid over to her older brother, her heart racing at the chance to join the game. Another chance to prove herself—or embarrass herself. Her feet fluttered away under the blanket as she tried to remember the strategies her father taught her for playing *pasur*.

Hagop dealt again and picked up his cards, showing them to Rosmerta. He pointed to an ace. "We'll play this one, okay?"

She nodded enthusiastically. Aghavni showed an ace and picked up the ten of diamonds from the tonir.

"Oh no! He beat us to it," said Hagop. "Now what?"

Rosmerta wanted so badly to show her worth. She examined each card, considering if it would help their cause. She couldn't see anything to play. She looked up at Hagop, befuddled.

"Not much to work with, is there?"

"No," Rosmerta agreed, glad at least that she hadn't missed something.

"We'll just put this one down, okay?" Hagop placed a queen with the other cards on the tonir.

"Thank you," snickered Aghavni as he collected the queen.

"Come on!"

"I think we made him mad," laughed Aghavni.

Anaguel giggled. "Why are they mad?"

"Because we're winning, and they don't like that."

"Why don't they like that?"

"Because they don't like to lose."

"Why don't they like to lose?"

"You ask a lot of questions, don't you?" Aghavni leaned into his daughter and tickled her. They both laughed.

Hagop rolled his eyes and played another card.

The game progressed with Hagop getting more and more irritated, while Aghavni and Anaguel got more and more boisterous every time they picked up a card.

Aghavni and Anaguel won easily.

"You're so lucky," Hagop said in exasperation.

Aghavni just shrugged.

"Papken, you're being very quiet. That's not like you," said Shushawn.

"Just thinking," replied Papken.

"That's not like you either," said Hagop.

"Okay, that's enough," chided Shushawn. "Megerdich will tell us a story, then we need to review our responsibilities for tomorrow."

"Papa, tell us about Tigranes."

Shushawn glared at Rosmerta with a cold stare of reproach.

Rosmerta quieted, her smoky green eyes peering through her frizzy mane of curly dark hair, pleading with her father.

"Haven't you heard enough about Tigranes?" asked Megerdich.

Rosmerta shook her head.

"Okay," he agreed. "The story of King Tigranes, King of Kings and greatest ruler of the Armenian Empire. Tigranes the Great was born 140 years before our Lord Jesus Christ as the crown prince of the Royal House of Artaxiad. After the defeat of his father's army by King Mithridates II of Parthia, Tigranes was sent to live in the care of the victors, where he perfected the ferocious military style of the Parthian generals."

"Especially the Parthian Shot!" exclaimed Rosmerta.

"Yes," laughed Megerdich as Shushawn scowled, "including the fierce Parthian Shot. Do you want to tell the story?"

Shushawn coughed. Rosmerta shook her head.

"When his father died in 95 BC," Megerdich continued, "Tigranes regained his freedom and took his rightful place as king of Armenia. At that time, Armenia was a loose association of various chiefs and small fiefdoms. Tigranes united them in one greater nation under his rule. He allied himself with Pontus and married Cleopatra, the daughter of King Mithridates VI.

"In 88 BC, Tigranes defeated the Parthians and took control of Atropatene and Mesopotamia, gaining him access to the Tigris and Euphrates rivers. At this point, Tigranes the Great took the title of King of Kings.

"In 83 BC, Syria chose Tigranes as their king. He went on to conquer Phoenicia and Cilicia. This was the pinnacle of the Armenian empire. Tigranes controlled the Mediterranean coast all the way down to Jerusalem, east to the Caspian Sea, and north almost as far as the Black Sea. Armenia had become the largest empire outside of Rome.

"In 69 BC, Tigranes' Greek mercenaries mutinied and allowed the Roman army to enter Tigranocerta. Lucullus, the Roman commander of the East, pursued the combined forces of Tigranes and Mithridates, but did not capture either King.

After sustaining heavy losses, Rome recalled Lucullus and replaced him with Pompey.

"In 66 BC, at the age of 75, Tigranes surrendered to Pompey. In recognition of his greatness, Rome allowed Tigranes to maintain most of his kingdom. Tigranes ruled as king of Armenia and ally of Rome until his death ten years later. And that is the story of the greatest of our people and the height we are capable of reaching. Never forget," Megerdich said, looking at his only daughter, "you come from greatness and you have that greatness in you." He moved the last few nuts to the center of a square piece of cloth he placed on the tonir. With a flourish, and the dexterity gained from years of practice, he flicked the cloth several times with his one hand until the nuts were packaged in a neat little satchel, which he handed to Rosmerta.

"Oh, you do spoil that child," Shushawn said. "Now we need to review our responsibilities for tomorrow. Come on, Papken, pay attention. We're doing this for you."

Wedding Preparation

Though he hadn't slept all night, Papken wasn't tired. He spent most of the morning pacing and arrived at the church an hour early. Once there, he paced some more. At one point, he stepped outside to do laps around the wooden building. Still, he did not feel tired.

Aghavni finally arrived, carrying the sheep. The animal was young and most days he could be found relaxing in the shade of the Bedrosians's courtyard. He was a friendly creature, who would often rub against a visitor's leg, or give a gentle head butt, hoping to be petted. But today he wasn't cooperating. Carrying him just seemed easier. Maybe the unfortunate creature understood what was about to happen. Maybe it found the unfamiliar streets distressing. Whatever the reason, he continued to squirm and buck in Aghavni's arms. Father Haig Kezerian said a prayer, and Papken tried to lead the sheep around the church.

Papken pulled on the rope tied tightly around the sheep's neck. He found that he was dragging the poor beast more than leading it. Eventually, he gave up and pushed the sheep from behind. When they reached the back of the church, Papken surveyed the long, fortified walls of Bayburt castle lining the ridge high above the town.

Papken's momentary distraction was all the sheep needed. It stopped suddenly, sending him tumbling to the ground. "Oh, you got me. Still, you know I'm going to win in the end." He got up and began pushing again. He returned to the front of the church to find Aghavni and Father Kezerian laughing hysterically.

Papken tried to ignore them and began his second circuit. When he finally completed his third trip around the church, Papken was relieved. He was anxious to get the proceedings under way. After all, he had more important things to do today. He dragged the stubborn animal outside the walls of the churchyard.

Aghavni and Father Kezerian joined Papken and his sheep. Father Kezerian made the sign of the cross over the sheep before pouring consecrated salt into a bowl and presenting it to the animal. The sheep, seemingly resigned to his fate, leaned forward and licked the salt. Father Kezerian looked up at Papken. "You broke him," he said.

Papken laid the animal on its back and tied his legs together. Feeling lightheaded, he took a deep breath and swallowed hard. He knelt heavily on the animal's body, firmly pushed its head away, and in one smooth and powerful motion, slit the sheep's throat. Blood soaked the ground. The sheep came to a quick end.

Aghavni took over from Papken, removing the rope from around the sheep's legs and chopping off its feet. Finally, he removed the animal's head. Papken went off to prepare for his wedding while Aghavni skinned the sheep.

The meat would be boiled in water with a little salt and distributed to the less fortunate people of Bayburt in an act of thanks for God's good grace and as a prayer for continued good fortune for the newlyweds.

Shushawn was responsible for preparing the food for the celebration. While she usually shared cooking duties with the other women, she took pride in creating these big meals on her own. She had done it so many times, she no longer needed to think much about what she was doing. With her hands chopping, kneading, and stirring on their own, her mind wandered.

Since the murder of her brother Bedros, she increasingly found herself reflecting on her life. Her first memory was of another celebration, when she was just a child. She wasn't sure what the event was, but she remembered seeing Aghavni. The boys were playing Long Donkey. Aghavni's team had just finished crushing their opponents back and was lining up for their turn. A small boy stood facing his teammates. Aghavni leaned over, put his head down, and wrapped his arms around the standing boy's legs. Another boy got behind Aghavni, bent over and wrapped his arms around Aghavni's legs. Each boy on the team lined up behind the last and braced themselves for the onslaught.

Seeing that Aghavni was the youngest on his team, the opposition chose their largest boy to climb onto his back. In succession, each of the opposing team's players climbed onto the back of one of the other boys. Aghavni never fell. In fact, after the boy behind him collapsed, Aghavni stood up, throwing his rider to the ground. His team had won. They jumped and yelled in jubilation. For some reason, Aghavni didn't join the celebration. He didn't boast of his obvious strength or even of defeating his opponent's strategy. He quietly walked away. Shushawn found it sad, yet somehow endearing. She watched him for the rest of the day. Occasionally someone would go over to speak with him. From a distance, the conversations seemed to be cordial enough. Often, there was laughter. Then, before long, Aghavni would be on his own again.

After a few of these encounters, Shushawn noticed something. When he was with others, Aghavni's left hand would slowly open and close. Not in a threatening way—and she was pretty sure Aghavni didn't know he was doing it—but steadily, repeatedly and unfailingly, his hand expanded and contracted as he talked. Then, when the conversation came to an end, and Aghavni was again alone, his hand relaxed.

As the party was winding down, a group of boys cornered Papken to tease him about his short stature. Aghavni quietly walked over to the group, his left hand hardening into a fist. He didn't attack…. He didn't even yell. Shushawn was concerned—there were at least eight boys against the two brothers. Yet the boys sulked away as if they were the ones outnumbered. Aghavni put his arm around Papken's shoulders and led him over to Hagop. The three brothers left the party, walking slowly towards their home.

A few years later, Shushawn sat against the wall of her house, while Megerdich and Aghavni talked with her father about the well he was building for the town. Aghavni knew every detail about the project. He even corrected her father about how deep they would have to dig. He was articulate and very intelligent. In spite of his obvious ability to contribute to the proceedings, Aghavni's hand was in motion throughout the entire discussion. When the meeting ended, the men stood and Aghavni turned to leave. As he walked away, Shushawn saw the hand cease its activity and rest by his leg.

At her wedding, Shushawn found it difficult to keep from looking at the ever-moving hand. She felt her eyes sliding down, then forced herself to look up at Aghavni's broad face. But at the edge of her vision...there it was...that hand...pulsing like an external heart.

A couple months later, Shushawn was sitting alone with Aghavni. There he was, calmly discussing their hopes for children, when she noticed that his hand was sitting motionless on his lap. In that moment, she knew that Aghavni was comfortable with her. She knew that she was in the right place, with the right man.

The Wedding

The sun slid in and out of the clouds, teasing the church grounds with light. A soft breeze caressed the town with the promise of warmer days ahead. Muhammad Kasaba stood at the gate to the churchyard, greeting guests as they arrived. It was unusual for a Muslim family to attend an Armenian celebration, but Muhammad was an exceptional man. He was the governor of Bayburt, and, as such, he figured he could go wherever he wanted. Who would say anything? And who cared if they did? Muhammad had been a close friend of Bedros Elmassian since they had worked together to get a new well dug for the town. He was outraged by the brutal murder of his friend, but was thrilled that his family had such a joyous event to keep them going amidst their grief. Muhammad knew that Emma had been Bedros's favorite.

On Muhammad's right, smiling broadly, stood his eldest son, Abdullah. Abdullah had been looking forward to this event for weeks.

Ahmet, Muhammad's younger son, stood to his left with his arms crossed, looking down at his shoes. He was humiliated. His buddies were harassing him about being friends with the infidel agitators. It was bad enough having the enemy living in the same town, but did he have to attend their events? And after the ceremony, he would have to visit them at the Bedrosians' home, a home that was nicer than the ones most good Muslims could afford. A home that should belong to a true Turk, not these conniving pagan thieves. Ahmet couldn't believe he was here. His friends would never let him live it down.

When the bride arrived, the Kasaba men walked into the church, took their seats at the back of the congregation, and waited for the service to begin.

Papken stood at the altar with Father Kezerian. His face lit up at the sight of his beautiful bride. Emma wore a traditional long dress and a scarf covered her head. She was radiant in the candlelight, and her luminous coffee colored eyes were as captivating as ever. A light breeze swayed the candle flames, highlighting the swirling, flower-petal-like pattern on the round medallion that hung from her neck. The effect was magical—as if the pendant was rotating. It had all been worth it. Papken and Emma had known each other their entire lives. Megerdich Bedrosian and his friend Bedros Elmassian arranged their union so long ago that Papken couldn't remember a time when he didn't know he would marry Emma. They had always been friends. Now they would be husband and wife. It was hard to imagine a better match.

Papken was in a daze through most of the wedding ceremony, but he refocused when the priest blessed them. It was time to exchange rings.

Papken and Emma turned towards each other. "Everyone's looking at us," whispered Papken.

Emma blushed, "Shhh."

The priest took Emma's right hand and put it in Papken's right hand.

Aghavni stood to Papken's side, holding a cross over the couple. The priest placed a copper crown on Papken's head and another on Emma's. Boy and girl, man and woman, husband and wife, and now king and queen of their own kingdom. When the ceremony ended, the whole congregation headed to the Bedrosians' house to celebrate.

Everyone, that is, except the bride and groom. Papken and Emma walked in the opposite direction to the Elmassian household, Emma's home since birth. There, Papken watched as his bride knelt down and reached into the cold tonir. With a twinge of regret for something familiar coming to an end, she scooped up a handful of ashes, placed them in a pouch her mother had set out for her, and slipped the pouch into her pocket.

"That's so dirty," Papken said.

"Stop it," Emma said. Then Emma and Papken walked back past the church and on to Papken's family home.

The newlyweds passed through the crowd gathered in the courtyard and stepped into the house. They walked three times around the Bedrosian tonir and then stopped and knelt in front of it. They bowed and kissed the wall of the tonir.

"Pfui," Papken spit out.

Emma rolled her eyes as she extracted the pouch from her pocket and sprinkled the ashes from her father's house into the tonir of her new home. She still felt the sense of loss, but it was accompanied by the excitement of a new beginning.

Papken and Emma squinted as they left the darkness of the house and entered the bright, sunlit courtyard.

Hagop and Aghavni ran to congratulate them, with Rosmerta close behind.

Papken raised his hand to his face to protect his eyes from the sun. "Married for less than an hour, and already she has me in tears," quipped Papken.

"I'm sure you deserved it," Aghavni retorted.

Hagop looked at Emma. "I hope he's not embarrassing you."

"Is he ever serious?"

"Not that I've seen," said Father Kezerian as he approached the group. "You did well today. Your father would have been very proud, Emma."

"Thank you. I miss him very much," she said, her voice trembling.

Rosmerta pushed through the men and hugged Emma.

"You're too sweet," Emma said as they embraced. "Who is that guy staring at us?"

"That's Abdullah. He's Muhammad Kasaba's son," said Aghavni. "I think he likes Rosmerta. He couldn't take his eyes off her when we visited Mr. Kasaba last month."

"Why were you visiting Mr. Kasaba?" asked Hagop.

"Megerdich and I were checking on the case." Aghavni didn't have to explain that it was the case of the man who murdered Emma's father. As Christians, the family had no right to be involved with the trial. However, as governor, Muhammad would know everything and pass any news along to his friends.

Rosmerta was happy to have the conversation shifting away from her. She glanced at Abdullah, trying not to be obvious about it. He was tall, with dark hair and intense, yet inviting, brown eyes. He had a long, straight nose and a broad mouth. He licked his thin lips and smiled at Rosmerta.

She looked away, then back, her head slightly tilted. She felt the heat rising in her face and moved slowly across the courtyard, away from her family.

Rosmerta slipped out of the courtyard.

Abdullah followed.

When she thought she was far enough away from the party, Rosmerta stopped and waited for Abdullah to catch up. She felt him approaching and turned and faced his broad and strong chest. Her eyes moved up his body until she gazed into his piercing brown eyes, her breath quickening.

Abdullah put his arms around Rosmerta, feeling the softness of her breasts pressing against his solar plexus. "I hoped we could find a moment to be alone today," he murmured into her hair.

Rosmerta nodded. "Me too," she said.

"I wanted to slip away with you last month when you visited with your father."

"Yeah," Rosmerta's heart was pounding now. She couldn't believe how nervous she was.

"I guess it wasn't the right time. Your family keeps such a close watch on you."

Rosmerta could feel Abdullah's hardness growing against her belly. She pulled him closer. "I know," she said.

Abdullah heard someone approaching and moved his hips away in embarrassment.

"Excuse me." It was Ahmet. "What are you up to, Abdullah?"

Abdullah pushed Rosmerta away, his hand hanging in mid-air in a bizarre display of shame, anger, and fear. "It's none of your business. Go back to the party."

"I don't think so. The party is boring. Now this, this is interesting. What are you doing with that filthy whore?"

"I'm not doing anything."

"Alright then, move aside, it's my turn."

"You have no turn."

Rosmerta tried to dodge the feuding brothers, but Ahmet grabbed her arm and pulled her towards him. "Let me go!" she screamed.

Abdullah stood there as Ahmet's hand slid down Rosmerta's back and grabbed her ass.

"That's enough," yelled Muhammad from the other end of the street. Ahmet shoved Rosmerta away and turned towards his father.

"Go home, Rosmerta," said Muhammad. "Abdullah, Ahmet, we're going home, too."

"But I have to walk Rosmerta back to her house," Abdullah protested.

"You've done enough. You both have. This is the first time in months that I've been able to relax and enjoy time with friends and you two have ruined it. Now do as I say."

Sulking, Abdullah did as he was told. Ahmet was gloating as they trudged away.

Rosmerta sprinted home, her shame growing with every step.

The Face Game

In spite of her misgivings, no one seemed to notice anything unusual when Rosmerta returned to the party. It appeared that nobody knew about her indiscretion—nobody in her family, that is. To her immense relief, everything seemed to be normal the next day.

Better than normal. Her yogurt was taken out of storage for the mid-day meal. It was a perfect thick curd with a slightly sour taste and smooth, creamy consistency. Rosmerta swelled with pride as Shushawn tasted the yogurt and brought it to the table. Shushawn ate with the men while the other women and children sat quietly against the wall. When the men finished, the women moved to the tonir for their meal.

They ate while the men were off doing whatever important things men do. When they finished, Rosmerta cleaned up the mess, then started mending a torn blanket. Shushawn stopped her. "Get the kettle and put it on the tonir."

When Shushawn instructed her to fill the kettle half full of water, Rosmerta felt a shudder of excitement. Was today to be the day she learned how to make tanabour?

"Now add two handfuls of the pearl barley."

Yes, this was tanabour. Rosmerta could feel the rhythmic beating in her chest quicken. She focused her attention on Shushawn.

"Now we wait for the barley to cook."

Preparing meals for the family was fun, but there sure was a lot of waiting. Waiting for the fire to light, waiting for the tonir to get hot, waiting for the water to boil and waiting for the barley to cook. Rosmerta didn't like waiting. She watched the grains swell as they absorbed more and more of the water, while her foot tapped rapidly on the floor, as if to keep pace with her heart.

Shushawn peered into the pot. "It's ready," she announced. "Put what's left of your yogurt into the other pot, add about the same amount of water, and stir."

Rosmerta did as she was told. She was uneasy as her yogurt thinned—she was sure she was ruining it.

"Faster," chided Shushawn. "Much faster. Pretend you're mad at it."

Rosmerta whipped the mixture furiously.

"That's better," Shushawn said. "Now set it on the heat and let it come to a boil."

More waiting, thought Rosmerta.

"Keep it moving. Don't stop stirring."

So much for waiting.

By the time the yogurt mixture was finally boiling, Rosmerta's arms were aching. She added the yogurt to the cooked barely and helped Shushawn remove the heavy pot from the tonir. They added sautéed onions, chopped mint, and parsley. After they'd let it sit for a few minutes, Shushawn grabbed a spoon, dipped it into the hot soup, lifted it to her mouth, and tasted. "A little salt," she said.

Rosmerta added a pinch of salt to the tanabour and looked up apprehensively towards Shushawn, who nodded encouragement. "A little more." She added another pinch. "That should do it."

Shushawn stirred the salt in and took another taste. "Perfect," she announced. "Next I'll show you how to make *chaimen* paste."

Rosmerta stood a little taller and tried to suppress a smile. Now, she just had to wait for the men to come home to eat the tanabour.

In the meantime, she played Anaguel's favorite game with her. Rosmerta pointed to the center of her face. "Nose," she said very deliberately, then she pointed to Anaguel's nose.

Anaguel giggled. "Rose," she said.

Rosmerta pointed to her ear, then to Anaguel's ear. "Ear," she said.

"Hear," replied Anaguel.

"Lip," said Rosmerta.

"Pop," said Anaguel.

"Pop? Pop doesn't rhyme with lip. What rhymes with lip?"

"Top," said Anaguel laughing uproariously.

"No," chuckled Rosmerta. "Come on, you're being silly. What rhymes with lip?"

Anaguel got very serious looking. "Lip," she said. "lip, sip, dip, hip, rip…"

"Okay, okay," Rosmerta said. "You're getting too good for this game. What else can we play?"

"Zip, blip, trip…"

"How about numbers? Do you want to play numbers?"

"One, two, three, five, nine, eight."

"No, I think you're getting tired. Are you ready for bed?"

"Bed, sled, head, tread."

"Wow, did she come up with that all on her own?" Megerdich asked as he entered the house.

"Yes," Rosmerta said. "She's excellent with words. We need to work on numbers, though."

"That's okay. She'll be a famous poet someday. Poets don't need numbers, do they, Anagueljan?"

Anaguel giggled and reached her arms out to her grandfather. Megerdich picked her up, hugged her close, and whispered in her ear. "You have a gift for words, just like my Anoush."

"Now don't you be exciting that child just before bedtime," said Shushawn. "Rosmerta, let's bring the food over to the tonir."

Rosmerta scurried over to help. She couldn't wait for her father to try her tanabour.

The Kasaba Family

"Stop it Muhammad. You've been pacing ever since you got home and it's driving me crazy," Yasemin said to her husband. She glanced at Abdullah sitting by the fire. He knew she wanted him to leave, but he stayed put.

"You haven't heard a word I've said," Muhammed said. "This is insanity. We can't do this to our neighbors."

"Muhammad," Yasemin said gently as she rested her hand on her husband's arm to calm his motion, "I *have* been listening, it *is* insanity, and you *can't* do it. Now sit down, and let's figure out what we *can* do."

Muhammad took a seat on the floor. Yasemin sat next to him and took his trembling hand. "Now, when is this action supposed to begin?"

"Now. As soon as I read the orders."

"How do they know you read the orders?"

"These were not regular orders. They arrived by special courier. He watched me open them, waited until I had read them, then took them back and destroyed them."

"Maybe you didn't understand properly. Maybe you thought the orders were preliminary and you are waiting for further instructions."

"No, Yasemin. The orders were clear. I know what I am supposed to do, and the ministry knows that I know. I have refused to obey. Now all I can do is wait to see what the government chooses to do about it. I don't imagine it will take long to find out."

"What do you think they will do?"

"To me? I honestly don't know. Eventually they will replace me with someone who will carry out the orders."

"Then we must warn the Elmassians."

"Warn the Elmassians of what?" asked Ahmet as he entered the house.

"The deportations," said Abdullah who was still watching his parents.

"Deportation? Here?" The excitement in Ahmet's voice was unmistakable. "It's about time. Those evil bastards have been taking advantage of us far too long. We created this great Turkish state, and they steal from us and get rich."

"The Armenians have never stolen from you, Ahmet," Muhammad replied with a note of exasperation.

"Oh, they haven't? We have to perform five years of military service. The Armenians pay a tax and avoid serving at all. While we're off defending Turkey, they take advantage of our absence to gain control of agriculture and trade. They get rich while we die protecting them."

"That's absurd, Ahmet," Abdullah protested. "Even if it used to be true, you know full well that all able-bodied Armenian men were conscripted into service last year."

"You're not fooling anyone, Abdullah. We all know you've got the hots for that devil Rosmerta."

"Rosmerta is not a devil!"

"You may be the oldest, dear brother, but you've got a lot to learn. The Armenians are tricky, scheming bastards who will do anything to steal from you, and if they get caught, they go crying to some foreign embassy that steps in on their behalf and gets them off. Where do you and I go if we get in trouble?

To jail, that's where. If we do something wrong, there are consequences. Now the Armenians have to face the consequences for years of taking advantage of Turkish hospitality. Well, I say it's about time the ungrateful, godless bastards finally get what they deserve!"

"Honestly Ahmet, I don't know where you learn this garbage," said Muhammad as he shook his head and got to his feet. "I'm going to pay a visit to our neighbors. We'll eat when I return." Muhammad walked past his son without looking at him. When he reached the door, he hesitated as if he was going to say something to Ahmet. His head dropped as he walked out into the cool night air without a word. His son was lost, but maybe he could save the Elmassians.

The Elmassian men were gathering for dinner when Muhammad arrived. After the customary greetings and requisite coffee, Muhammad and Margos got down to business.

"I was deeply saddened by the decision in your brother's case," Muhammad said. "Life in prison is more than he deserves. Kaj Mohmod is an animal who should have been put to death."

"And he would have been, if Bedros had been a Muslim."

"That is true. My friend, I fear the injustices to your people do not end there. I apologize, Margos; I come with grave news."

"You're being very formal, Muhammad. Is this an official visit?

"No, far from it. In fact, if I had done my official duties, this conversation would be too late. My orders were to begin the deportation of all Armenians from Bayburt starting tonight. Margos, my friend, I am here to warn you that you must take your family and escape from here immediately."

"Escape? Escape to where? This is my home. I was born and raised in Bayburt." A sudden shock of fear tightened Margos's chest. "Where do you suggest we go?"

"Ultimately, nowhere in Turkey will be safe. You must leave the country. For now, I would recommend that you travel west. Stay ahead of the insanity and you might manage to save your family."

The men embraced. Muhammad returned home. After explaining the situation to his immediate family, Margos went to his sister, Shushawn, and the other Bedrosians.

By the time Margos reached the Bedrosian household, dinner was over and they were settling down for the night. A couple years ago, they would have stayed up longer, but since the Balkan war, kerosene was too expensive. The whole town went dark early. Margos arrived to find Megerdich sitting quietly in the courtyard. The men moved into the house to discuss what Muhammed had told Margos. Their arrival woke baby Megerdich. Adelina tried to go to the baby, but at eight months pregnant, she found it difficult to get up. Hagop tried to help her but ended up falling on her.

When things finally settled down, Margos reported the news from Muhammed. The objections were immediate.

"Ever since our brother, may he rest in God's good peace, was killed by that maniac, you have been paranoid," Shushawn said dismissively. "How could they evacuate the whole town? You know Armenia was the first country to declare itself Christian. God will not allow it."

"God has already allowed it, Shushawn. Zeitun was evacuated two weeks ago."

"Then the people of Zeitun must have done something to have offended the Lord. We are good Christians here in Bayburt; no such thing will happen to us. Even you say that Muhammad Kasaba has refused to allow it. Besides, look at Adelina. She's in no condition to travel."

"And neither am I," said Megerdich. "I'm an old man, and I've seen the Turkish culture of massacre before. Your God did not help my Anoush, and he will not help you. You need to take everyone who is healthy enough to travel and get out of here. I'll stay behind with those who cannot."

"No," said Shushawn. "This is our home. We shall stay here and let God's will be done."

The finality in her voice disappointed Margos. They argued for a while longer, but to no avail. He shook his head and left. He had done what he could.

First Life

The next morning, Margos loaded a cart with everything they would need. He tethered his donkey to the cart and got his family ready to go. He made one last visit to the Bedrosians. There was no swaying them.

Rosmerta was scared. Megerdich had always been an attentive father, and though she had never known her mother, Shushawn had been a good surrogate. To see the two of them so at odds with each other left her feeling vulnerable. "Maybe we should go, Shushawn," Rosmerta suggested meekly. "Papa and Uncle Margos seem so certain."

"You are wise for your years, Miss Rosmerta. How about you come with us?" said Margos.

"Absolutely not!" Shushawn cried. "We will not split up the family. Margos, if you want to run in fear, that is your business. We will stay here. God will see to our safety."

It was decided. Margos went back to begin his family's western migration.

Rosmerta was unsure about staying in Bayburt, but she was glad she wasn't being separated from her father. She could see that Megerdich was anxious, and that upset her. "Help me with my French," she said.

"French? What good is studying French going to do you now?" chided Shushawn.

"It will keep our minds busy," Megerdich said quietly.

Armenian was the preferred language at home, but conducting business with the local Muslims required Turkish. Everyone in the Bedrosian household spoke both. Western

European languages were only spoken by the better educated people in the Ottoman Empire. Especially in the rural eastern provinces, most of the better educated people were Christian. Megerdich had been teaching Rosmerta French since she was a baby. She no longer needed much help; she was practically fluent. Shushawn didn't want to learn, so Rosmerta often found excuses to switch to French whenever she wanted to have Megerdich to herself. No matter how crowded the room, she and her father could share some time to themselves.

Megerdich loved this time with his daughter almost as much as she did. It was during these times that he taught Rosmerta how to collect water from a running stream, how to start a fire in the rain, how to use shadows to tell which direction you were moving and the approximate time. He showed her how to make a satchel out of a towel. But mostly, it was a time to tell Rosmerta about his life.

In spite of his calm exterior, Megerdich had never fully recovered from the atrocities he experienced in what he called his first life. Most of the family didn't want to hear about it. It wasn't that they were insensitive to Megerdich's suffering; they just didn't want to dwell on the dismal tale anymore. Rosmerta, on the other hand, loved to hear her father's stories. A quick switch to French, and Rosmerta could enjoy time with her father; the rest of the family could ignore the whole thing.

Megerdich loved to tell his daughter about their people's past. He often started with the Russo-Turkish War. After the defeat of the Ottoman forces in 1878, stories circulated about Armenians in Eastern Anatolia changing sides and fighting with the Russians. While the rumors were clearly overblown and mistakenly applied to people and even entire towns where they were not accurate, they were not entirely unfounded. In truth, there were small elements within the Armenian community that could only be described as revolutionary. However, with the exception of a few notable groups, most Armenians were peaceful, loyal servants of the Ottoman Empire.

Conditions deteriorated in Eastern Anatolia after 1890 when 125 Armenian Russians, led by Sarkis Gugunian, invaded in an effort to help their compatriots. They were supported financially by wealthy Ottoman Armenians. Their forces were poorly supplied and too small to be effective. The invasion was quickly repulsed.

Rumors of further Armenian intrigue circulated around Eastern Anatolia, resulting in unrest and the deaths of hundreds of Armenians. Meanwhile, with encouragement from the powers of Europe, Armenians were calling for equal treatment under the law, as called for in the treaties that ended the war with Russia.

Already regarded as paranoid, Sultan Abdul Hamid II took advantage of the situation. Kurdish tribesmen were making life difficult for Armenians. Hamid encouraged, and at times assisted, them in their efforts.

While the troubles in 1895 were still the result of rumors about Armenian plots, the circumstances were vastly different from just a few years earlier. Rather than spontaneous civilian mobs, the brutality of 1895 was supported, orchestrated, and often carried out by soldiers of the empire.

Megerdich and his young bride Anoush had been expecting their first child when it happened. He was in the market when the shooting started. A group of men entered from the north end of town and fired shots into the Armenian-owned shops. Shopkeepers and shoppers alike fled, leaving everything behind. Megerdich hurried home to protect his wife and their unborn child. He sprinted through the market and around the public square, and past the old wooden church where people were already gathering. It seemed that most of the Christian population of Bayburt was seeking safety in the house of God. But Megerdich continued running until he reached his house at the end of Yavuz Street.

It was still quiet in the Armenian section of town. People heard gunfire in the distance but didn't want to admit to themselves what it meant. "It's started!" yelled Megerdich as he burst through the door. "They are attacking Armenians. Everyone is gathering at the church. We have to go."

Megerdich's brother Abraham immediately grabbed his wife and their six-month-old daughter and headed for the church. Megerdich found it difficult to get his almost full-term wife moving. Anoush leaned heavily on him, puffing and panting as they made their way to the church less than a mile down the road. When his family was safe inside, Abraham went back to help his brother.

Two of the attackers saw Abraham leave the church and ran after him. A shot was fired. A bullet whizzed by Abraham's head as he joined Megerdich and Anoush.

"Well, what do we have here?" asked the man who fired the shot. He was dressed like a Kurdish tribesman, in the traditional baggy pants, with a red vest over his white shirt and a blue turban. A large, bushy mustache completed the costume. Megerdich knew that Kurds did not usually carry weapons affixed with bayonets, and the hair peeking out from under the man's turban indicated he was not Kurdish. Bayonets meant Turkish soldiers. This was a government action. The man's companion wore similar clothing but was armed with only a sword.

"What do you think, Aziz, a boy or a girl?" the man with the bayonet asked.

"It's obvious, Erol. She's carrying very low, almost dragging the poor thing on the ground. Got to be a girl," said Aziz grabbing Anoush by the arm and pulling her towards him.

"No!" Megerdich yelled, as he tried to hold her back.

Aziz swung his sword and cut deep into Megerdich's shoulder. The blade stopped only when it hit bone. Megerdich released Anoush and fell to his knees clutching his shoulder in disbelief.

Abraham ran towards Megerdich. Erol stepped forward and drove his bayonet into Abraham's chest while Anoush fell backwards beside him. Abraham thrashed about at the end of Erol's rifle for a moment, then became still.

Anoush was lying on the ground looking up at Aziz. Erol pressed his foot on Abraham's chest and tried to retrieve his bayonet. It wouldn't budge. "Damn!" he cried. "What a waste." He fired a shot into Abraham to release his weapon from its trap. "Now, where were we? Oh yes, I remember. You believe that this bitch is carrying a female mutt, is that right?"

"Yes," replied Aziz.

"I'm afraid I must disagree. I think it is a male dog she carries."

Megerdich lunged from his knees towards them, but Aziz kicked him in the head, his boot slicing a deep gash in Megerdich's cheek.

Anoush started to crawl away. She gave up when Aziz brought his sword to her throat. "What is the wager?" he asked.

"One lira."

"Very well, let's find out." Aziz rotated his sword in an exaggerated sweeping motion starting from Anoush's neck. The blade swished high over her body and down in a hard, chopping motion, cutting deep into her swollen abdomen. Anoush tried to scream but only managed a gasp. Aziz reached into her belly and pulled out a fetus. "I told you so—female."

Megerdich rose to his feet and stumbled towards his wife. Aziz swung his sword again, slicing deep into Megerdich's skull. Megerdich heard screaming. He was surprised to realize it wasn't coming from himself. He was shocked to see the church on fire.

Murad Tarik came running towards Megerdich. "Hurry," he said to the attackers. "You're needed at the church. They're trying to escape." The two men ran off. Anyone who escaped the fire was pushed back into the flames with a bayonet or, failing that, shot dead outside their place of refuge.

Murad, a Muslim doctor and a longtime friend of the Bedrosian family, carried Megerdich to his house and hid him for several weeks while things returned to some semblance of normal. Megerdich survived with a bad scar on the right side of his face and an area on the top of his head that never again grew hair. Murad was forced to remove Megerdich's left arm. Otherwise, Megerdich returned to good physical health.

The town took longer to recover. Many of the Armenian homes burned to the ground. Most of them were stripped of all valuables and anything else useful, including food. The market area was almost totally plundered. Over twenty percent of the Armenian population was dead. It would have been much worse except that many Muslims hid their Christian neighbors during the attacks. Bayburt's road to recovery was long.

Boghos Elmassian

Margos returned home to find his wife screaming and crying hysterically. She was flailing about so much that she almost knocked Margos off his feet when he tried to hold her. "Boghos!" she screamed. "Taken!"

"Calm down, Margaret. I can't understand you when you're like this. Boghos was taken? Taken by whom?"

"Ahmet Kasaba. He came with a gang of boys... at least ten of them... all armed with cudgels. They threatened to kill us if we tried to stop them. There was nothing..." She began to sob uncontrollably.

"It has started," Margos muttered under his breath looking up to the sky. He lowered his gaze and looked deep into his wife's eyes to address her tenderly but firmly. "Of course there was nothing you could do. However, there is something I can do. Margaret, you need to pull yourself together. Ani and Rozin need you. The cart is loaded. You must start the journey without me. I will go and get Boghos. We'll catch up with you before the sun sets. Are you ready?"

Margaret nodded, still shaking from fear or rage. She wasn't sure which—probably both. She loaded her girls on the cart and began the long journey to Sivas, a city about 200 miles west of Bayburt. It would take them about a week to get there. And then... and then what? It didn't matter; it was time to leave. Past time.

Margos found Muhammad Kasaba preparing for a trip of his own. "Where are you going?" he asked.

"Erzurum," Muhammad said. "Official business. What's wrong? You look upset."

Margos hesitated.

"What? What is it Margos?"

"It's my son, Boghos. A group of boys kidnapped him from our home."

Muhammad stiffened. A fleeting look of shock crossed his face, replaced almost immediately by anger. He clenched his teeth. "Ahmet?"

Margos nodded.

Muhammad took a long, slow, unsteady breath. "I'll take care of this. You need to take care of Margaret and the girls. I'll get Boghos and we'll catch up to you. Where are you going?"

"Sivas."

"Good. You need to get going. We'll be right behind you."

The men embraced and parted ways. Muhammad knew where to find Boghos. He had followed his son several times and knew the abandoned farmhouse just outside of town used as a hideout by Ahmet and his band of thugs. The previous inhabitants were Armenians who left town several months ago.

When Muhammad barged in through the front door, he saw his friend's teenage son lying on his back, held down by four of Ahmet's accomplices. Ahmet was kneeling at the boy's head chanting verses from the Quran.

"Stop!" screamed Muhammad. "Boghos, come here. Ahmet, go home now. The rest of you, get out of here."

Boghos was crying and a high-pitched whine was coming from deep within him. Muhammad felt sorry for him but didn't have time to comfort him. He grabbed Boghos by the arm and led him out of the house into the midday sun. They walked back towards town and then continued west to catch up with the Elmassians.

Shortly after losing sight of Bayburt, a group of Ottoman soldiers approached them on horseback. "You're going the wrong way, governor. Son, you should go," said one of the men.

Muhammad nodded. Boghos ran in the direction the man was pointing—back towards town. As he ran, he heard a single shot from behind him. It took a while before Boghos understood that he was alone. His family was on their way to God knows where, and he had no way of getting to them. Shortly after sunset, he left his empty house and went to see the Bedrosians.

After Boghos told his story, Megerdich let out a long sigh. "So, it is true. It is to happen again."

"Oh, don't be so dramatic," said Shushawn. "When Margos realizes that Muhammad isn't coming, he will return for Boghos."

"I hope not," said Megerdich. "Muhammad Kasaba is dead. Soon, a new governor will be appointed, and then we are all in trouble. For tonight, we are stuck here, and Boghos is our guest. Rosmerta, get him a blanket. It is time we got some sleep."

Rosmerta retrieved a blanket from the stack against the wall and carried it to Boghos. She could see that he was upset and a little nervous. "Don't worry," she said. "We'll take care of you."

"I don't need anyone taking care of me," Boghos snapped as he snatched the blanket from her.

Rosmerta recoiled.

"That's enough," said Megerdich in a tone that made it clear there would be no more squabbling.

It was time to sleep.

The Disappeared

The day had been warm, but it cooled off quickly at night. Rosmerta could hear Boghos sobbing in the corner. Otherwise, there was no noise. Rosmerta thought she heard sounds in the distance—footsteps maybe. She decided it was her imagination. She was about to fall asleep when the door swung open with a deafening crash.

"Allahu Akbar!" shouted the men as they stormed into the house. There were seven of them, all armed with pistols. Megerdich recognized one of them as Aram Khan. Aram seemed to be a decent fellow when he worked as a police officer at the market in Erzurum where Megerdich was selling his grain, but Megerdich knew that everything would be different now. He rolled towards Rosmerta to get between her and the charging gendarmes.

"No need to worry, Megerdich," Aram assured the old man. "We're not here for you."

Panic squeezed Rosmerta like a band tightening around her chest. She couldn't understand what was happening. She watched the officers move through the house, rolling people over and pulling off their blankets. "Over here, I've got one," yelled a young officer as he put a choke hold on Hagop.

"Me too," yelled another as he yanked the covers off Papken.

Aghavni jumped up behind the young gendarme holding Hagop and punched him hard in his kidney. The man collapsed, gasping for breath. A shot rang out, and Aghavni fell back against the wall. Then his legs gave out, and he crumbled to the floor clutching the fatal wound in the middle of his chest. His face showed a moment of terrified understanding, then went slack. He fell onto his side and was quiet.

"We don't need any more heroics tonight. Take them," Aram said, indicating Hagop and Papken.

"No!" screamed Emma, the blood draining from her face. She stood up, only to be thrown on her back by one of the gendarmes.

"What about this one?" asked the policeman holding Boghos.

"He's too young," responded one of the others.

"Okay, just those two then."

Emma tried to stand again. Adelina grabbed her arm and held her down.

The gendarmes left with Hagop and Papken.

Shushawn rushed to Aghavni. Her scream filled everyone in the house with a shocked panic followed by a gut-wrenching feeling of sympathy and dread.

Emma finally managed to stand, and Rosmerta thought she was going for the door. Before she got there, Emma grabbed a blanket from the floor and threw it against the wall. She then started running back at Adelina. This time she practically threw herself at the wall, her arms flailing away as if to punish it.

Rosmerta ran to Emma and wrapped her arms around her waist. Emma's thrashing subsided. With one last, harrowing scream, she collapsed to the floor. Emma's hands were cold and clammy, her heart pounding hard enough for Rosmerta to feel it.

Megerdich went to Shushawn and put his arm around her shoulders. She was crying and shaking violently, her hands moving furiously over her husband's body as if she was trying to put him back together.

"Is he dead?" Shushawn asked.

Megerdich put his hand on Aghavni's chest. "Yes," he said. "I think he is."

She looked at Megerdich in desperation. "Why?"

"There are no reasons for things like this. You know that. He was a good man, Shushawn. A good grain merchant, a good husband, and a good father. He didn't deserve this. But now you must think about your children. Anaguel and baby Megerdich need you to be strong. Do you think you are up to preparing the body?"

Shushawn nodded and wiped her face with her sleeve.

"Very well," said Megerdich. He removed his arm from Shushawn's shoulder and reached down to close Aghavni's eyes. "You'll have to clean him, and you'll need binding cloth," he added in an attempt to get Shushawn started on her task. Megerdich rolled Aghavni onto his back and stretched his body out with his legs together and arms by his side.

"What will they do to the others?" Adelina asked nervously. "What do we do now?"

Megerdich stood, moved to the door, and stepped into the courtyard. He walked past the peach trees and peered out. Men were coming and going out of houses up and down the street. "I don't know what will happen to the men, but the village is crowded with gendarmes and there is nothing we can do tonight," he said when he went back inside.

"But Aghavni is dead!" cried Shushawn.

"Yes, and Papken and Hagop will likely be dead before sunrise."

An unworldly shriek came from somewhere deep inside of Emma. Her scream reignited the panic in everyone.

Rosmerta started shaking. It felt as if the air had left the room.

"It looks as though they are arresting all able-bodied men," Megerdich continued, trying to suppress his own grief over the loss of his sons in order to keep the others calm. "That will keep them busy. I don't think they'll be back tonight unless we do something stupid. Let's calm down and..."

"What about you?" shouted Shushawn. "Why didn't they take you?"

"I'm hardly able-bodied, and I would guess I'm too old even if I were. And you heard the gendarme, Boghos is too young. But I'd be surprised if he were too young by very much. You'll want to be careful, son."

"Yes sir," Boghos whispered.

Rosmerta rushed to her father and wrapped her arms around him. "I'm scared," she cried.

"Me too," said Megerdich. "Now let's sit together and pray for Hagop and Papken and for the soul of our dearly departed Aghavni."

"Yes, pray," said Shushawn. "Now that's something we can do."

"Lord, in these dark days, let us remember our hero Saint Sarkis," Megerdich began. "He was a great general in the Greek Army. So great that he became a general to the Roman Emperor Constantine. He fought bravely and won many battles. But it is not for his military conquests that we remember him. He destroyed many pagan idols and constructed churches where pagan temples once stood. But it is not even for this that we remember him. When Julian the Apostate became emperor after the death of Constantine, Christians were mercilessly persecuted and suffered tremendously. Jesus appeared to Saint Sarkis and told him that like the patriarch Abraham, he must leave his land and travel to a new country. Saint Sarkis obeyed the command of our Lord and traveled through Armenia and on to Persia.

"After winning many battles as the commander of the Persian army, King Shapur heard that Sarkis was proselytizing in the name of our Lord Jesus Christ. He became enraged and called Sarkis to the palace. He demanded that Sarkis worship before the pagan gods. Sarkis refused. So, King Shapur killed Sarkis's son Mardiros. Even so, Sarkis would not bow before the false gods.

"At his own execution, Sarkis preached the word of God one last time and asked those gathered to see him die if they too would accept Jesus as their savior. Then Sarkis was martyred. Lord, we pray that we too will prove to be strong enough to stand up to those who persecute us, and that, like Sarkis, we will never forsake you even in these dark days. For we know that if ever we find ourselves in grave danger, Saint

Sarkis will intervene to help us. This we pray in the name of our Lord Jesus Christ. Amen."

"Amen," everyone repeated.

"Shushawn, you should get started."

Shushawn knelt beside Aghavni's body. "Get me some cotton sheets," she instructed Rosmerta. "And I'll need some water and a few towels as well." Megerdich had positioned him well, but one of his eyes had popped open. He appeared to be winking back from the other side. Shushawn closed his eye. She cut a strip of cloth from the edge of a towel and tied it around Aghavni's face to keep his mouth shut. She cut a couple more strips, each more crooked than the last.

"I'll do that for you," Rosmerta offered.

"No!" Shushawn exploded. "I'm doing it."

Rosmerta ran to her father and tried to disappear in his lap.

Shushawn finished cutting the ragged strips and started undressing Aghavni. She removed his baggy trousers and set them beside his hat and boots resting near where he slept. She slid his vest over his shoulders and tried to pull it down behind him. The weight of what she was doing overwhelmed her and she fell beside the body. She sat up and tried again, yanking on the vest in frustration. She glanced up at Megerdich, who nodded his encouragement.

Rosmerta went back to help. Shushawn was tense and was breathing hard at the exertion. Working together, Shushawn and Rosmerta removed Aghavni's vest, then cut off his cotton shirt.

With gentle strokes, Shushawn cleaned the blood from her husband's chest. She hesitated before removing his underwear. The smell told her what she would find, and she didn't want everyone seeing Aghavni like this.

Under normal circumstances, everyone would leave while a wife undressed and cleaned the body of her husband. Shushawn knew that was impossible tonight. She steeled herself and exposed him. Aghavni was a mess of urine, blood, and feces. Using a wet towel wrapped around her hand, Shushawn quickly washed him off and set the towel aside. Rosmerta took the messy cloth and threw it into the courtyard.

Shushawn sat back, her hands shaking violently. She realized that Megerdich was right; she had to be strong for the children. She wrapped another wet towel around her hand and washed Aghavni's middle, set the towel down, and used a corner of the linen to cover his private parts. Then she washed Aghavni's head, his hair, face, and beard. Next, she washed the right side of his upper body, then the left side. She washed his right leg and finally his left leg. After each section of the body, Rosmerta disposed of the dirty towel.

The cleaning ritual was meant to be repeated two more times, but Shushawn was running out of towels, so she used the last one to dry the body. She laid three sheets beside the corpse, one on top of the other, and turned towards the others. "I need help lifting him," she said.

Boghos and Rosmerta obliged, moving the body over the sheets laid out on the floor while Shushawn pulled on the corners to keep them taut. Once the body was on the material, Shushawn reached for Aghavni's left hand. It was cold now.

This surprised her. She had been so concentrated on the task of cleaning him that she hadn't stopped to think much about what she was doing. Suddenly, the meaning of all this activity hit home. Aghavni was dead. Anaguel and baby Megerdich no longer had a father. Shushawn no longer had a husband. Her wonderful, handsome, quirky Aghavni was gone. Tears welled up in Shushawn's eyes. Rosmerta went to her. Shushawn pulled away. She wanted these last few moments with her husband, her man, her Aghavni.

After regaining most of her composure, Shushawn tried again to move the left hand of the corpse—it was no longer Aghavni—over the chest. The arm didn't move easily, but she managed to get it in place. She placed the right hand on top of the left.

She picked up the edges of the top sheet and folded it over the body. "In the name of the Father," Shushawn said. She repeated the folding process on the second sheet— "and of the Son,"—she folded the third sheet around the body— "and of the Holy Spirit."

"Amen," said Megerdich from the corner of the room.

"Amen," agreed Shushawn. She took the remaining strips of cloth, tied one around the sheets above the head, one below the feet, and two around the middle.

Shushawn was exhausted. She backed up against the wall and slid down into a sitting position, not realizing how similar the move was to when Aghavni met his end. She sat there weeping.

Boghos retreated to his sleeping place. He was shaking noticeably, trying desperately not to cry.

Rosmerta's instinct was to provide comfort, but after the blanket incident, she was afraid of Boghos. She didn't know what to say to him anyway.

Then Emma broke down. She had been sitting quietly, watching Shushawn preparing Aghavni's body. With that finished, she was left to contemplate the fate of her husband. It started as a high-pitched squeal and grew into a loud moan and finally a wailing scream. Rosmerta ran to her and fell into her lap.

Emma quieted and held Rosmerta as tightly as she could. Rosmerta felt Emma's medallion pressing against her head. She pulled back and looked into Emma's watery eyes. Emma lifted the charm by the necklace so Rosmerta could get a good look at it. Even in the dim light, it was beautiful. Eight sickle-shaped forms emerged from a point in the center, each one succeeding the last, in an everlasting circle. A raised edge marked the outer rim of the pendant. Rosmerta held it, staring at it in awe.

"My mother gave that to me just before my wedding," Emma sighed. "It is an *arevakhach*—a symbol of eternity." She sobbed.

Suddenly, Boghos howled as he stretched himself violently out of a fetal position. Megerdich slid beside him and said something Rosmerta couldn't hear. Now they were all crying.

The family spent the rest of the night praying, crying, and trying to comfort each other. Sleep was hopeless. When the sun came up, Megerdich and Bedros left the house to see what else happened during the night.

Megerdich had been right. All able-bodied Armenian men between about 18 and 45 had been taken. Among them was Father Kezerian.

Training

The sun was hot on the inmates' faces. Kaj was soaked with sweat, though he had regained control of his breathing. Training was going well. Kaj wasn't sure what was expected of him. All he knew was that he was to be transferred to the mountains in the Caucasus, and whatever they wanted him to do there, it had to be better than jail.

The training was physical—running and smashing things with sticks. Kaj liked that. Twice a day, they were called to attention and some high-ranking fool would yell at them. Kaj settled in to listen to today's speech, figuring that was the price he had to pay to be part of the Special Organization.

The speaker's voice was strong, with a deep resonance that rumbled through Kaj's bones. The speaker seemed to believe what he was saying. He became more excited as he reached the primary point of his speech.

"Our forces were decimated and our people suffered, but it is not our failure. It was not some great victory for our Russian enemy. We were betrayed by a cancer from within. The Armenians have repeatedly created uprisings to incite the Turks, and then after enough force has been used to suppress them, they cry oppression and elicit the sympathies of the European powers. This time, they've gone too far. Not only did the Armenians force us into a war with Russia, but many of them ran to the Russian side to fight against us. And with what aim? To steal the very heart of our great nation and create an Armenian state on our Turkish land! Already they have perpetrated the most heinous atrocities against our people.

They have butchered and massacred entire villages, taking the spoils for their own vile purposes.

"We are surrounded by enemies. By taking away Greece and Romania, Europe has cut off the feet of our beloved Turkish state. The loss of Bulgaria, Serbia, and Egypt has deprived us of our hands, and now by means of this Armenian agitation, they want to get at our most vital places and tear out our very guts. This would be the beginning of total annihilation, and we must fight it with all the strength we possess.

"They call the Ottoman Empire 'the sick man of Europe.' But our sickness is not a mystery. It has a name. It is a parasite called Armenians. If we have learned anything from our losses it is that we cannot tolerate outsiders on our land. It is Turkey for the Turks. We must cleanse ourselves of this sickness. That is our mission. When we have completed our work, there will be no Armenian question.

"Our Turkish race is older and superior to all others. We are more intelligent and stronger. Among our many gifts to the world are civilization and tolerance—too much tolerance for our own good. Our forefathers were feared the world over for their conquest of the infidels. Our ancestors shed their blood so we could have so much. It all started with Ertaghrul's 400 horsemen. It continued with the early Sultans, Osman, Orhan, Murad, and Bayezid. There was Mehmed the Conqueror, who delivered the unmatched city of Constantinople to us in 1453. And of course there was Suleiman the Lawgiver whose greatness is even recognized in the West, where he is remembered as Suleiman the Magnificent.

"All of these great leaders made one major miscalculation—a mistake that has caused the undoing of many of their great triumphs. They did not destroy the infidel Christians when they first conquered them. Therefore, today, in Anatolia at least, we must correct this oversight. Today, we begin to cure the sick man. And in doing so, we ensure the success of Islam over its enemies. We shall save Turkey for the Turks, and we shall no longer coddle the infidels. The iron fist of the Turk shall take hold of the world again, and the world shall again tremble before it! As you do your work, always remember that the surest way to heaven is to kill a Christian. Allahu Akbar!"

"Allahu Akbar," came the reply. The inmates were screaming and thrusting their arms in the air. They were ready. They were transferred the next day and given their final instructions before they headed into the mountains as the newest regiment in the Special Organization.

Funerals

A cold, gray sky drizzled moisture onto a gloomy scene at the Christian cemetery near the church. Boghos and a couple of teenagers from town dug a grave, while Megerdich supervised. The pile of dirt sat precariously by the edge of the hole. The four men walked back to the house to retrieve the body.

Shushawn was praying over Aghavni's body when they arrived. "Are you ready?" she asked, hoping in a strange way that they were not.

"Yes," replied Megerdich as he and the boys entered. The three young men lifted the body to shoulder height and proceeded out of the house. Shushawn stayed behind. Women did not attend funerals. Megerdich followed the procession to the cemetery. The ceremony was unusually short. A priest from across town agreed to help in Father Kezerian's absence. There were many funerals, so he could only spend a short time at each.

The men lowered Aghavni into the grave. Large stones were placed on top of the body. Megerdich considered the sheet-wrapped body of his eldest son. He had lost two wives, an unborn daughter, and now this. He let out a short gasp as he took a handful of dirt from the pile and dropped it into his son's grave, saying, "Ashes to ashes." He grabbed another handful and let it fall. "Dust to dust." And a third handful of dirt. "The Lord bless him and keep him. The Lord make his face to shine upon him and be gracious unto him and give him peace." With each phrase, Megerdich seemed to slump a little lower.

The three boys then shoveled the rest of the dirt into the hole. Megerdich and Boghos walked back to the house in silence. The teenagers stayed in the graveyard to help other families bury their loved ones.

It was traditional to have a party after a burial. Friends and relatives of the deceased would gather for an extravagant feast and dance long into the night. But things were not normal in Bayburt. Every Armenian family was trying to determine what happened to the men who had been taken during the night. Most had at least one funeral of their own to organize.

While Aghavni was being buried, Shushawn, Emma, and Rosmerta prepared a meal for the men. They knew that it would be a small gathering. The rest of their family had left town and everyone else they knew had their own problems. Even so, the tonir was covered with the traditional funeral fare of kidney beans, as well as bread, consommé, savory pies, fish, pheasant, artichokes, salads, and fruits.

But when Megerdich and Boghos were nearing home, there was a big commotion. Instead of entering the house for the feast, Megerdich told the women to follow him out. They all headed towards the town center with the rest of Bayburt.

Most news arrived in Bayburt through a makeshift network of rumors and hearsay. Much of this information turned out to be inaccurate. People usually didn't mind the falsehoods; gossip was a source of intrigue and entertainment. But there was an official source of news that people relied upon, especially in times of distress. So when the town crier, Ibosh Assad, was seen walking towards the town center, word spread quickly, and a large crowd began to assemble. The entire gathering fell silent the moment Ibosh raised his hand and began to speak.

The war, it seemed, was going well. There had been a minor break in the Turkish lines and the Russian army was approaching the area. Nothing the great Turkish army couldn't handle, but Bayburt would soon be engulfed in conflict. For the safety of the citizens, everyone was being evacuated to secure areas away from the fighting.

"The Armenians will be evacuated first," Ibosh explained. "The Armenian men have already been taken to the secure zone, where they are setting up new homes for your families. In seven days, those of you who are still in Bayburt will be transported to join them. Each family should prepare a list of the property and possessions you will have to leave behind. Those lists should be delivered to the town hall, and arrangements will be made to compensate you for what you cannot take with you. When you arrive at your new homes, each family will receive a parcel of land, housing, agricultural equipment, seed grain, and supplies necessary to get started. The journey will take three days. Plan and pack accordingly."

"A week to prepare for leaving our entire lives behind? It's not enough!" someone shouted.

"Perhaps you would like to stay behind and explain that to the Russians," Ibosh responded.

"What about the Muslims? Why can they stay?"

"The process of evacuating Bayburt will take time. We must begin somewhere, and we will begin with the Armenians. You have one week to prepare. I suggest you use it wisely," Ibosh said, as he pushed his way through the crowd. Many questions followed him. He kept walking and repeating, "One week."

"Well, that's not bad," said Shushawn. "We have a week to get ready, three days of travel, then we get a new farm and get back to work. A hassle, but not too bad."

"Shushawn, they stormed into our home unannounced and killed your husband," Megerdich pointed out. "They took Hagop and Papken. Would any of that have been necessary if the evacuation story was true? You can't possibly believe they will give us a new home."

"Then what are they going to do with us?"

Megerdich just shook his head and looked away. "I don't know."

"None of us know," said Adelina, "but we need to prepare for a journey, so let's prepare. I'll start making the bread."

The bread was hard biscuits. There were still a few peaches left over from last year's crop. Megerdich told Adelina to make sandwiches. She said it was too soon, but he insisted. Sometimes it was just easier to do as Megerdich said, even if it didn't make sense.

Boghos went back to his old house to scrounge for anything useful he could find. He found nothing. His mother had been quite thorough when she packed.

When he returned to the Bedrosians, Boghos helped Megerdich repair a cart so they would have something to transport their supplies. There were constant disagreements about what should stay and what should go. The big, black kettle had been in the family for as long as anyone could remember. It had served them well and Shushawn insisted it had to go with them. Adelina was equally convinced that they needed to travel light, and this huge kettle was too heavy for such a trip. The kettle's weight did not keep either woman from moving it into and back out of the "to go" pile each time the other left the room.

Over the next two days, there were many such arguments about what to bring and who would be responsible for carrying it. On the third day, word came that the Armenians would not be allowed to take their animals. Without the mule to pull the cart, the kettle issue was resolved. Adelina helped Rosmerta load the kettle onto the repaired cart and harnessed it to the mule. Rosmerta headed into town to sell the kettle. After about an hour with no luck, she walked past the Kasaba boys.

Ahmet seemed amused. "Why would we buy anything from you? Next week it will be ours for the taking." He laughed explosively as he walked away, leaving Abdullah alone with Rosmerta.

Abdullah fidgeted nervously and looked everywhere except at Rosmerta. "I need to talk with you," he said.

"Okay," she said, trying to meet his eyes as he scanned the horizon behind her.

"I'm sorry about all that stuff at the wedding."

"It wasn't your fault." She considered adding some thoughts about whose fault it was, but decided against it.

"I'm sorry about the deportation stuff, too."

"That's not your fault either."

"I know, but it isn't right."

"Sorry Abdullah, I'm kind of busy. I really need to get ready." She couldn't bring herself to say, "to leave."

"Oh yeah, right. Well, it's just that… I mean, I was wondering… We have plenty of room, and it's not going to be easy for you to travel and… Well, I would take care of you, and my father said it would be okay—before he died, I mean—and my mother… Well, she doesn't know, but I'm sure she wouldn't mind. She knows how father always liked your family."

"What do you want, Abdullah?"

"I want us to get married," he said simply, then waited for a response. After a short pause—though it seemed like forever to him—Abdullah continued, "You won't have to leave Bayburt. You can stay and live with us."

"And the rest of my family? What about my father? We can all stay with you?"

"Ah…no. I mean, just you. We will be husband and wife and you will be safe from whatever it is the government has planned for the rest of your people."

Rosmerta frowned. "I'm not staying here while my father and Shushawn are driven away from me. And what about Adelina? She's pregnant. She'll need help to keep up. I can't abandon her."

"Yeah, okay, fine," said Abdullah. "So, goodbye," he added, as he turned away. He was embarrassed about being rejected, yet somehow relieved. In fact, as he walked away from Rosmerta he realized he hadn't wanted her to say yes. Marrying a Christian girl would make things difficult. Sure, she would have converted. Of course, everyone in Bayburt would know who she was and that she wasn't really one of them. And there was Ahmet to consider. His brother's hatred for the Armenians scared him. It was probably for the best that she said no. Yes, definitely for the best.

Rosmerta walked away wondering if she had made the right decision. She didn't want to leave her family. Still, she couldn't help thinking about what might lay ahead for them. Whatever it was, she had just dismissed the last opportunity she would have to avoid it.

Deportation

Rosmerta woke to see Shushawn lighting the fire. She got up and went to help with breakfast. She filled a pot with cold water from the bucket and ground the coffee. She added the coffee grounds and some sugar to the pot and brought it to Shushawn, who placed it at the edge of the fire. While the coffee heated, Rosmerta placed another pot of water at the hottest part of the tonir. Shushawn served up the yogurt. Breakfast would be ready as soon as the men rose. All that was left to do was the bread.

The starter for the *lavash* had been left to rise overnight. Rosmerta added flour and some of the heated water. She kneaded the ball of dough, rolling it towards her then pushing it away. By the time it was smooth and elastic, her arms were aching. She tore off a piece and flattened it into a nice round piece of sweet, earthy smelling dough. She stretched it over a hay-filled cushion and handed it to Shushawn.

With a flourish, Shushawn pushed the cushion behind her, swung it over her head, and pulled it towards her with all her strength, sticking the dough firmly to the inside wall of the red hot tonir. She quickly pulled the cushion out and set it aside.

From somewhere outside, a loud scream reverberated through the house, startling them all. Half awake, the men looked at each other in confusion. Then there was a banging on the outer courtyard door. By the time Rosmerta could get there, it swung open and two gendarmes yelled, "Everyone assemble at the town square in one hour!" The door slammed shut and the gendarmes were gone.

Megerdich jumped to his feet. "Shushawn, get the food. It is time to go."

"It can't be, we still have four days! They said we had a full week to prepare. They can't do this."

"Oh, stop it, Shushawn. They can do whatever they want. Now get the food. Boghos, get blankets. Rosmerta, you help me with other supplies."

The Bedrosians gathered their small collection of transportable belongings. Except for Megerdich, who used his one arm to lean heavily on a cane, each family member wrapped their share of the load in a blanket that was tied onto their back. The blankets could be used for bedding or to fashion an impromptu tent. The very pregnant Adelina carried enough wooden sticks to form two tents. In addition to carrying baby Megerdich, Shushawn carried most of the food, which amounted to several days' worth of dried biscuits, onions, and barley they could use to make soup, along with some sandwiches and a few apples. Emma had a frying pan and a heavy pot for the soup. She was also responsible for keeping track of Anaguel. Boghos carried one change of clothes for every member of the family and a supply of small rags to keep baby Megerdich in diapers. Rosmerta carried two clay jugs for collecting water and a special gift from Megerdich.

While the others were gathering their things, Megerdich took Rosmerta into the courtyard. They sat under the peach tree and he told his youngest child about his worst fears. "Remember the story of Sarkis?"

"Yes," Rosmerta said. "St. Sarkis refused to renounce his faith even under the most dire circumstances."

"That's right. And what happened to Sarkis because of his refusal?

"He was martyred for our faith."

"He was killed. That's right. And many more will be killed soon."

"But St. Sarkis will protect us. Won't he?"

"No, Rosmerta," Megerdich said, looking into his daughter's innocent eyes and wishing that he did not have to say these things. "Sarkis will not protect us. It looks as if we will soon be going on a journey. I am an old man. I will not be able to keep up with the caravan for very long. You will have to go on without me."

"But Papa . . ." Rosmerta protested, fear growing in her voice.

"No buts. Just listen. I will protect you as long as I can. When the time comes that I no longer can, St. Sarkis will not defend you. And if there is a God, he will not protect you either."

"But Shushawn says…"

"Shushawn's faith is admirable. She is a real St. Sarkis, who will die for her faith. Let Shushawn have her God, but you must be ready to take care of yourself. Can you do that?"

"Yes," Rosmerta said weakly. She was very confused.

"Rosmertajan, there may come a time when you don't know what is the right thing to do. There is only one thing you need to consider. Whatever keeps you alive is what you must do. Don't worry about anything else. Do what you must to survive. When there is life, there is hope. Do you understand?"

"Yes," Rosmerta said again.

"Good." Megerdich pulled a square of red silk from inside his jacket and spread it out on his lap. He reached back into his jacket and took out a small silver comb. The sun glistened off the comb in a dance of sparkling light. Its ornately decorated head was a cluster of cherry blossoms cradled in an arrangement of exquisitely formed leaves. "Do you know what this is?"

Rosmerta's eyes widened. "Is that the comb that Anoush was wearing when…"

"Yes, on that horrible day. And I want you to have it." He placed the comb in the center of the square of red silk, then grabbed the opposite corners and tied them together. "Tie this onto the belt under your shift to hide it. You will need it later."

"Yes, Papa."

"Rosmerta, you will soon discover that when circumstances allow it, some people can be very cruel. Others can be very kind even when it is dangerous for them to show kindness. You need to be able to tell one from the other. Don't let your expectations or religion blind you to the truth of who is on which side. Don't worry about St. Sarkis. Don't let Shushawn push you into doing something stupid because she has faith that God will protect you. You must take care of yourself. Do you understand?"

Rosmerta nodded. It didn't make any more sense on the second telling.

"I hope so," said Megerdich. He had done what he could. He hoped it was enough.

Megerdich and Rosmerta joined the others and they all headed for the center of town. Emma sniffled as they passed the church that had so recently been the site of such joy. Several men were standing at the door, as if guarding the drawbridge of a medieval castle. A mother approached them, shooing her children into the church.

Shushawn stopped. "People are congregating here. We should join them."

"No," is all Megerdich said. He kept moving.

Rosmerta rushed to his side. Emma hesitated, then continued on, leaving Shushawn holding baby Megerdich in front of the church.

Shushawn looked back and forth between the refuge offered by the wooden building and the procession of people shuffling towards the town square. She called out to Anaguel, who was still with Emma. "Come to Mama, Anaguel."

"Keep walking," ordered Megerdich.

Emma reached down and swept Anaguel into her arms. "We need to stay together, Shushawn. Come on, we're going."

Shushawn waited a moment more, then exhaled in exasperation and jogged to catch up.

The town square was crowded with clusters of apprehensive-looking Armenian families.

"I want to go home," said Anaguel.

"Not yet," Emma answered. "We need to be patient."

"What are we doing?"

"We're waiting for the police to tell us what we are supposed to do. We'll be on our way soon."

"Where are we going?"

"I don't know. We just have to wait. We'll know soon. Look, here they come."

Sixty gendarmes rode up to the edge of the crowd on horseback. Among them, Rosmerta saw Aram Khan, one of the men who had seized her brothers that terrifying night. He said something to the nearest group of people and two gendarmes started off with the families closest to them following. The remainder of the gathering fell in line and started moving away from the rising sun.

Before long, the entire Armenian population of Bayburt had formed a line of humanity, walking with the few possessions they could carry. Over 5,000 people made up the mile long procession. The recent rains turned the road out of town into a boggy trail of mud. The bottom of Rosmerta's dress was soon coated with black gunk. Her shoes were soaked. After two hours of walking, the gendarmes at the front stopped. The line compressed to a halt and everyone waited for instructions.

"Listen up, folks. We know that you were forced to leave your homes before you were ready. This action was necessary because of increased enemy activity. Since you may not have had time to prepare enough food for your journey, we have arranged to distribute food to you. I need for the senior male in every family to follow me to collect it." Aram Khan turned his horse and headed off to the north.

Boghos started after the gendarme, but Megerdich grabbed his arm. "I am the oldest in this family group," he said with a smile.

"In your family," Boghos corrected, "and I am the oldest in mine."

"No, we are one family group, and I will go."

"They're giving away food," Shushawn said. "Surely an extra ration will help us."

"No, Shushawn," said Megerdich, his voice tight. "They're looking at us. One of us has to go. I don't think anyone will be returning with any rations." Megerdich left before he finished speaking. Boghos stayed behind.

Some 400 men wandered off with ten gendarmes. Fifty gendarmes stayed behind with what was left of the Armenian families. The men walked over a small hill and disappeared from view.

"Where are they going?" Anaguel asked.

"They're going to get food," Emma responded, trying to hide her fear.

"I'm hungry."

"I know, sweetie. We'll eat soon."

A shot rang out.

Rosmerta's head swung around to see Shushawn jump. "What was that?"

Now Anaguel and baby Megerdich were crying.

There were screams and more shots from behind the hill. Then the gendarmes returned. They were alone. The procession resumed without the men. The mood was somber. No one spoke. They just walked.

When the sun reached the horizon in front of them, the caravan stopped. The travelers began their preparations for the night.

Boghos and Shushawn unfolded the sheets to set up a tent while Rosmerta grabbed the jugs and went to look for water. There was a small stream running behind the camp. Rosmerta walked upstream looking for a place where the water was flowing quickly over a smooth rock as Megerdich had taught her. It pained her to think of her father; she still couldn't believe he was gone. It was only earlier today that he had warned her that she would have to go on without him. That time had come much sooner than she expected.

Rosmerta found the perfect spot and filled the two jugs. Then she picked up one in each hand and turned to see Aram Khan looming above her on his black stallion. She wondered how long he'd been watching her.

"You're very pretty, little miss. What are you doing out here all by yourself?" Aram asked as he dismounted.

"I'm collecting water for my family."

Aram moved towards Rosmerta. He reached out to touch her face, making sure his hand brushed her breast on the way there. "It's not safe for a little girl to be out here alone."

Rosmerta took a quick step back and lost her footing. She tumbled seat first into the stream, shattering the jug in her left hand. She was sitting in the cold mountain stream holding one full jug and the handle of another as she stared at a man she did not know and did not trust.

"Oh, I'm sorry," said Aram, thoroughly embarrassed. "Are you okay?"

"Oh yes, fine," lied Rosmerta as she pulled herself back to her feet. "I really must get back with the water. Well, what's left of it."

"Yes, of course," said Aram, returning to his horse. "I must get back as well. Are you sure you're okay?"

"I'm fine," Rosmerta insisted. She waited by the side of the stream until Aram rode out of sight. Then she began the slow climb up the muddy embankment. A sharp pain shot up her leg every time she stepped on her right ankle. She was limping badly, but she didn't think she had broken anything.

"Just walk it off," she knew Megerdich would have told her. And it seemed to be working. By the time she got back to the camp, her ankle was feeling a little better. Rosmerta joined Shushawn and her children in their tent. Adelina and Emma were already asleep in the other tent. Boghos had wandered off. Rosmerta entertained Anaguel with the face game, while Shushawn put baby Megerdich to bed.

Shushawn was very concerned when she heard what happened at the stream. Rosmerta hadn't planned on telling her, but she needed some excuse for returning with only one jug of water, and she was too tired to make up anything as convincing as the truth.

Shushawn grabbed a blue shawl from her meager belongings and handed it to Rosmerta. "Here," she said, "In the morning you should rub dirt on your face and wear this. It will make you look older and less appealing. Try to pass yourself off as an old lady and the men won't bother you."

Rosmerta doubted it would work, but she took the shawl. Night fell quickly. It had been a long and stressful day. After eating, Rosmerta spread a blanket out and lay on her side. Something sharp dug into her. She rolled over. The comb. Anoush's comb. Megerdich had told Rosmerta the story of his first wife so many times that she knew it by heart. Yet, it was always a story of the past, ancient history to Rosmerta. Until now, that is. It seemed somehow more real, more relevant, now that Rosmerta had left her own "first life" behind and was beginning another chapter in the ever-expanding story of her family. Where would it all lead? What was to happen to them? It was only this morning that they left Bayburt. The only home they had ever known already seemed very far away.

Night Terrors

At the base of the mountains, some two miles ahead of the Bayburt caravan, another group was preparing for the night. The horses were ready and the officers' weapons were loaded. Kaj had finished sharpening a sturdy knife and the short, curved blade of his sword over an hour ago. He was beyond impatient when the order finally came to move out. The soldiers moved at a slow jog, just fast enough to warm up in the cool night air, with the officers ahead of them on horseback.

The easy descent made for a quick journey requiring very little exertion. The path sloped gently through a wooded area, then the trees began to thin and they came into a clearing, where Kaj saw hundreds of tents. The captain gave the sign, and Kaj stopped with about a hundred of the troops. The other half of the men charged forward.

The first group of soldiers ran through the rows of tents, grabbing the peaks and pulling the canvas behind them, leaving the stunned occupants exposed and disoriented.

Then another signal instructed Kaj's group to proceed with the second onslaught. Kaj charged into the camp, swinging his sword wildly at anyone who raised their head.

Rosmerta heard the commotion from her tent in the back of the camp, furthest from the oncoming attackers. She went to the opening at the front of the tent. Shushawn grabbed her arm and begged her not to go. Boghos jumped up and disappeared through the opening before anyone could react. There was a deafening chorus of screams in the night. Outside, it was the noise of people being cut to pieces. Inside the tent, it was baby Megerdich and Anaguel screaming in horror at the sounds of slaughter.

A few minutes later, Boghos returned. "We have to leave."

"Leave? And go where?"

"It doesn't matter. They're killing everyone. The only reason we're not already dead is that they started at the other end of the camp. Now come on, we have to go." What remained of the Bedrosian family followed Boghos away from the camp. They were not alone. Many others were moving out of harm's way.

From their hiding place in the woods outside the camp, Rosmerta couldn't see much. She could hear heart wrenching screams of agony ripping through the night, sending waves of terror through her. Her muscles tightened, pulling her body into a ball. While her vision was still compromised, the sounds were unmistakable—blades swooshing through the air, bones cracking, and constant screaming. These sounds would never completely leave Rosmerta's ears.

The Special Organization forces butchered the hapless Armenians until they heard the call to retreat. Reluctantly, Kaj joined the unruly procession back to the mountains.

Rosmerta didn't see the attackers depart, but the screams died out and were replaced by moaning. "We should go back and see if we can help."

Boghos agreed. He started back toward the camp, followed by the others. The scene was horrifying. Many of the tents were on fire, lending a ghoulish orange light to a scene of mass murder. There were babies clinging to their headless mothers. Body parts were everywhere—a hand here, a leg there. When Rosmerta got to the center of the carnage, she couldn't move for fear of stepping on someone. She saw a baby with a hole through its belly and remembered Megerdich's stories of soldiers throwing infants in the air and catching them on their bayonets.

Rosmerta heard a low moan from behind her. She turned to see a pregnant woman trying to stand. She ran to the woman's side and tried to help her up.

"My baby! Is my baby okay?"

"Yes, your baby's fine," Rosmerta said, hoping it was true. The woman was covered in blood. Rosmerta searched the woman's body for wounds and found none. The blood didn't seem to be hers. The woman's name was Hauteur Adrian. She was from Erzurum and had been visiting her sister in Bayburt when the deportation order came. With no way to get back to Erzurum, Hauteur was deported with her sister's family. Now she was the only member of her party left alive.

Rosmerta was still working to get the blood cleaned off Hauteur when the sun rose. It was only now, in the light of day, that the horror of the previous night was fully visible. The whole camp was covered in blood. Body parts were strewn everywhere, and mutilated corpses were piled on top of each other.

The gendarmes approached from the west, spreading out in a line around the campers. Aram Khan ordered everyone to pack up. "It's time to get out of here."

"Where were you last night?" Boghos demanded as Aram rode past.

Aram ignored the question and kept going. Behind him, the people packed what they could and began another day of walking.

The Cliff Face

Rosmerta was glad to leave the killing field behind. She dreaded what was ahead, but was too busy to think much about it. Shushawn was carrying Megerdich and holding Anaguel's hand. She found it difficult to keep up with the procession. Megerdich was heavy. She carried him for a while in her right arm then stopped, shifted him to her left arm, moved Anaguel to her other side and started again. It wasn't long before Anaguel got tired of the game, and Shushawn was more or less dragging her daughter behind her.

Rosmerta could not help Shushawn. She had her hands full assisting two pregnant women. Hauteur was relatively healthy—she was scared and depressed, but in spite of everything, physically intact. Rosmerta encouraged her to think of her baby and keep going.

Adelina, on the other hand, was absolutely exhausted from walking. Her back was screaming at her as she shuffled her feet forward, ever forward. Breathing hard, she leaned heavily on Rosmerta.

Boghos and Emma were left to carry all the provisions for the family. They had left the tent behind and carried only the food and some supplies necessary for starting a fire, a long-handled frying pan, and a large copper pot.

The Bedrosian family was bringing up the back of the caravan. The gendarme leading the group had long ago disappeared into the distance. He reached the end of the gentle uphill grade and instructed his followers to head up a steep path that would take them over the mountain. The gendarme started working his way back along the line, prodding people to keep moving. He assured them that they would soon be able to rest.

Aram Khan tried to talk with Rosmerta from his position at the rear of the caravan, but she was too busy to carry on much of a conversation.

Boghos, on the other hand, kept questioning Aram. "Who were those people last night? Where were you when they were killing us? Aren't you supposed to be protecting us?"

Aram ignored Boghos at first, then told him to shut up and keep moving. Finally, in exasperation, he fell back and waited.

Then he saw his partners riding towards him from the front of the line. "They're moving too slowly," one of the gendarmes complained. "We'll need to keep up the pace if we're going to make it in time."

"Yes, sir," replied Aram.

Aram joined the other gendarmes and rode away, back in the direction of the killing fields.

"Where are you going?" yelled Boghos. "What the hell is going on?" When the gendarmes disappeared, Boghos stopped. "Come on," he said. "We need to get out of here." Boghos could see that they were coming into a clearing with a cliff ahead. He could barely make out those at the front of the caravan climbing the steep rock face. Boghos moved the Bedrosians off the trail and into a small clump of trees.

The Captain's choice of campsites for the night had seemed rather strange to Kaj. After completing their mission, the Special Organization returned to the clearing at the base of the cliff. It had worked for one night, why not stay there again? But the Captain ordered them to follow the stream along the base of the cliff for another mile until they reached a second clearing. The site didn't have anything going for it that the first one lacked. The decision to move didn't make much sense. But he was the Captain, so that was that. After setting up his tent, Kaj fell asleep almost as soon as he lay down. He didn't stir until the wakeup call. He was well rested and ready to go.

They broke camp slowly. Apparently there was no hurry for their next mission. After a midday meal, a scout came into the camp to speak with the Captain, and soon after, the Special Organization forces were called to formation. They began their march back along the stream, towards their original camp. Before reaching it, they spread out and charged a group of Armenians who were beginning to climb a steep cliff. Kaj ran into the middle of the horde. He and his compatriots formed a wall dividing the mass of people in half, then turned and worked their way to the front of the pack now trapped by the cliff before them.

Hidden in the trees, Boghos watched in horror as the Special Organization once again slaughtered the defenseless Armenians. The attackers were charging through, swinging heavy sharp blades seemingly at random. Arms and legs were strewn about with the rest of their owners' bodies lying beside them screaming. Occasionally, a well-aimed saber would slice clean through a neck, decapitating the victim in an instant. Most of the wounds brought death more slowly. Many bled to death, sometimes in minutes, sometimes hours. The soldiers kept moving, swinging and slicing one victim after another.

Adelina screamed from behind Boghos. She was going into labor. Rosmerta tried desperately to calm her. Shushawn was busy controlling her two children while Hauteur cried quietly at the base of a tree.

Boghos went to help Rosmerta. "What do I do?" he asked.

"Talk with her, try to quiet her down."

Adelina screamed and grabbed Boghos with all her strength, tearing into his flesh. While the massacre continued at the base of the mountain, Adelina gave birth to a bloody mass. The baby was dead. Rosmerta wrapped the baby in the blue shawl Shushawn gave her and quickly carried it away. She left the body in a small depression and started back to check on Adelina.

Before reaching the safety of the trees, Rosmerta saw Aram returning from the other direction. "Are you hurt?" he asked, with what under other circumstances might have been taken for genuine concern.

"No," Rosmerta said, looking down at her blood-soaked shift.

"I'm glad to hear it," he replied. "We need to get moving." Aram went to the front of the caravan, leaving another gendarme to keep the group from falling too far behind.

"Where were you this time?" chided Boghos to the new gendarme.

"That is none of your concern. Now get back on the trail and get moving."

"We need time to tend to the wounded," protested a young woman bandaging her son's bloody leg.

"You have no wounded," the gendarme said as he reached for his belt. He raised a small handgun and shot the little boy in the head. The woman screamed and charged the gendarme. He adjusted his aim and put a bullet into the middle of her chest. "Now get moving," he said to the rest of the stunned crowd.

Rosmerta went to get Adelina. Shushawn gathered the children while Emma and Boghos collected their depleting supplies. Soon they were back on the trail. It turned out they would not be climbing the cliff face after all. Instead, the remnants of the Bayburt Armenians followed the stream that ran along the cliff. As they passed the recently dead, Rosmerta noticed that none of the bodies were wearing any jewelry. In fact, many were stripped to their underclothes, and some were entirely naked. Had the killers taken the time to remove the valuables from their victims? Or was it other Armenians taking what they could? She decided it wasn't worth thinking about. In the moment that Rosmerta wasn't concentrating on what she was doing, Adelina fell to her knees. She struggled to pick Adelina up, pulling with all her might. Her strength was gone. Adelina didn't budge.

"Get moving, you two."

"She can't, she just gave birth. She needs time to recover."

"That's not my problem. Now get moving."

Rosmerta surveyed the area, looking for help. She couldn't see anyone she knew. There was nothing but a long procession of humanity moving away from her.

"Now!" yelled the gendarme.

Rosmerta gave one powerful heave, and Adelina was on her feet again. She threw Adelina's arm over her shoulder and pulled her forward. They started to move again.

They passed an elderly woman sitting on the side of the path muttering to herself. Rosmerta wanted to help her, but she had her hands full. She kept moving and the old lady was left to the elements.

Rosmerta had dragged Adelina for almost a half hour when they came to a small clearing. She couldn't know that they were passing through what had, a few hours ago, been the camp of the men who had slaughtered so many of her people. The Special Organization forces had long since disappeared into the mountains.

Halfway through the clearing, Adelina's will gave out. She stopped and fell to the ground. Rosmerta was dragged down beside her. "Come on, Addy, we have to keep moving. The camp is not far ahead. You've made it this far, come on." It was no use, Adelina was spent. There was a loud crack, and then Rosmerta saw blood flowing from Adelina's back.

"Get up and get moving, or you're next," said the gendarme in a tone that suggested he was merely saying hello to a passing friend.

Rage exploded in Rosmerta. She screamed and pulled Adelina's body to her. She saw the gendarme point his weapon at her. Then her father's voice came back to her, calm and reassuring: *"You must be ready to take care of yourself."*

Rosmerta got up and rejoined the others. She passed enough people to make sure she wasn't at the end of the line where the gendarme might decide she was holding up progress. Shaking with rage, she was weeping openly. She was beyond caring what anyone thought.

And then, in a flash, as if someone struck a match in a dark room, Rosmerta realized she was alone. Not totally alone—she was surrounded by people—but she didn't know any of them. She walked faster, working her way through the line, looking for anyone she recognized. Rosmerta's stomach dropped and panic filled her chest.

After two more hours, the caravan came to a stop. Rosmerta gave up on finding anyone and began looking for a place to spend the night when Boghos appeared in front of her.

"Where's Adelina?"

"She's dead," is all Rosmerta could manage. "Where's everyone else?"

"Most of us are over there," he said pointing into the mass of people. "But we can't find Anaguel."

"What do you mean you can't find her?"

"Emma and I went ahead to stake out a place to spend the night before all the best spots were gone. Shushawn couldn't carry Megerdich and drag Anaguel at the same time. She was forced to leave Anaguel on the side of the road. I don't think she made it to camp and the asshole gendarme at the back won't let us go and look for her."

Rosmerta followed Boghos to their campsite. She couldn't believe what she had heard. If Anaguel was on the side of the road, then she must have walked right by her.

Shushawn was sitting by the fire crying and staring into space.

Emma was seated beside Shushawn, holding baby Megerdich. "Anaguel was lost on the trail. Shushawn was running around screaming her name for almost an hour. Her voice just gave out."

"That's what Boghos told me, but it can't be true. I was at the end of the line when they killed Adelina. I couldn't have passed Anaguel and not recognized her."

"That family over there said they saw Shushawn at the end of the line arguing with the trailing gendarme. The gendarme told Shushawn to move or be killed. She couldn't carry both Megerdich and Anaguel. She had to leave one of them. The lady over there said she couldn't help because she had two children of her own. Shushawn left Anaguel in the middle of the road screaming. She carried Megerdich here, left him with me, and searched the camp looking for Anaguel."

Now Rosmerta was outraged. If this was true, she had to have passed not just Anaguel, but Shushawn struggling with the two children. What was wrong with her? How could she have not recognized them? If she had found Shushawn, she could have helped, and Anaguel would be with them. How could she be so stupid? And what about Hauteur? Had they left her alone back where Adelina delivered her baby?

Rosmerta sat by the fire Boghos had started. She pulled her knees up and buried her face in her thighs. She blinked hard, trying to stop her tears. It was no use.

Boghos sat beside her and put his arms over her shoulders. "It's not your fault," he assured her.

Rosmerta looked up and tried to speak. No words came.

"We'll find them."

Rosmerta turned away. "No, we won't."

He wanted to tell her she was wrong—assure her that everything would be okay. But he knew she was right. Nothing was certain anymore. He changed the subject. "You know we're betrothed?"

Startled, Rosmerta's head jerked back to face him.

Boghos blushed and looked away.

"Yes, I know," said Rosmerta. "I guess that doesn't matter now."

"I guess not. But who was that guy at the wedding?"

"What guy?" Rosmerta asked, wondering why she was having this conversation.

"When you left the party—the guy who followed you. The Muslim boy."

"Oh, Abdullah Kasaba. I was trying to get away from him."

"It didn't look that way. It looked as if you were trying to be alone with him."

Rosmerta snorted.

"There was a second boy who followed you," Boghos prodded.

"That was Abdullah's brother Ahmet. He's a real asshole."

"I know. He tried to kill me. If his father hadn't arrived when he did, I'm certain he would have." Boghos told Rosmerta all about the attempted execution in the house at the edge of town.

As she listened, Rosmerta couldn't help going over what happened to her on Papken's wedding day. The more she thought about it, the more upset she got. Ahmet called her a whore, and Abdullah didn't defend her. He didn't do anything. She knew he was afraid of his brother, but he said nothing. Maybe Abdullah was the real asshole.

Rosmerta realized that Boghos knew who the two boys were all along. "What brought all of this on anyway—our betrothal, and the Kasaba boys, and all? What does it matter now?"

"That first night I stayed at your house—the night your brothers were taken—your father said something to me. He reminded me that I was to be your husband and told me that I would have to take care of you. But then I remembered the boys at the wedding. I didn't figure you wanted me to take care of you."

"Well, you weren't too thrilled when I told you we would take care of you, either."

"That's true," Boghos admitted. "I'm sorry I yelled at you."

"That's all behind us. I just wish I knew what's ahead."

"Yeah," agreed Boghos. "Where are they taking us?"

"I don't know. Wherever it is, they're not going to make it easy for us to get there."

"That's true, Rose. We need to work together if we're going to get out of this."

Rosmerta's eyes widened in disbelief.

"I'm sorry. Do you mind my calling you 'Rose?'"

She hesitated, then replied, "No. It just surprised me, that's all. Actually, I like it."

"Good. I like it, too. I guess we should get some rest."

It was a long night. Without the tent, it was cold. They spent a lot of energy trying to keep the fire burning. It went out anyway. Rosmerta couldn't sleep. She kept going over the terrible series of events since leaving Bayburt. The men disappearing over the hill, the senseless attacks, Adelina's baby, Adelina's death, and losing Anaguel. And what happened to Hauteur? And now to discover that Boghos had almost been killed! It was all too much.

When the sun rose, the gendarmes assembled the Armenians and they started out again. They were going into the mountains.

Mountain Trails

The trail was hard and rocky. Rosmerta and Shushawn took turns carrying Megerdich. Emma and Boghos were again hauling the supplies. The women stayed together with the baby while Boghos darted ahead. As they climbed higher and higher into the mountains, more and more people simply gave up and sat at the edge of the trail waiting to die. Those with the strength to keep going shuffled past them, trying not to make eye contact. No one looked back.

The mountain air cooled as the sun sank to the horizon. When they stopped for the night, Rosmerta grabbed the jug and went to get water. She felt a tingling sensation in her fingertips, as if she was picking up a loaded pincushion. She ignored it and wandered off the trail to find a stream. By the time she returned to the camp, her hands were worse.

Emma fixed a meal from the last of their supplies. After dinner, they found a flat spot on the ground and tried to sleep. Rosmerta curled up into a fetal position and began to moan. She was shivering violently. The tingling in her hands would not let up. While it wasn't exactly painful, it was certainly uncomfortable. If only her father was here. He would know what to do. Rosmerta's moans grew into a fit of uncontrollable sobbing as she thrashed about, trying to get warm.

Emma slid over to Rosmerta. "What's the matter?"

"I'm cold."

"I know, honey. We're all cold."

"Yes, but my hands hurt."

"It might be frostbite. Let me help," said Emma, as she moved Rosmerta's hands to her abdomen. "Wow! They *are* cold," she exclaimed. She engulfed Rosmerta in a hug and tried to warm her up.

Rosmerta's flailing stopped as she allowed Emma to consume her in warmth. The embrace was comforting, but the cold was unyielding. She jerked up into a sitting position. "Where is your medallion?"

"One of the gendarmes stole it."

"When?"

"A couple days ago. It's nothing. Don't worry about it. Come on." Emma pulled Rosmerta back to her.

Boghos watched from a distance, not sure what he could do. He curled up in a ball and tried to ignore the sounds of Rosmerta's torment.

After a couple hours, Rosmerta's whimpers subsided. She was still awake and shivering. The night was quiet except for the chattering of her teeth. No one got much rest.

Shushawn spent the night curled up with Megerdich, doing everything she could to keep him warm. The baby was wrapped in a heavy wool blanket.

When morning finally broke, there was nothing to eat. Boghos disappeared before they started the march and the others didn't see him again until the end of the day.

The trail into the mountains began with a steep ascent. Shushawn was exhausted, and the baby was heavy. She set him down on the trail, breathing hard. "I can't. I just can't."

Megerdich just stood there, his arms outstretched to his mother.

"That's okay," said Rosmerta. "I'll carry him."

"No, you had a rough night. You need to take care of yourself. I'll carry Megerdich," said Emma.

Her objections came too late. Rosmerta had already picked him up. She was shocked to find that she couldn't feel the rough texture of his wool blanket. The pressure from the baby's weight brought out a general numbness in her hands. Her fingers felt swollen. She checked and saw that they appeared normal except for a disturbing lack of color. She shifted Megerdich to her left arm and raised her right hand to her face. It was cold against her cheek, but she could feel nothing in her hand.

Rosmerta's core body temperature increased once they started hiking, but that still didn't help her hands. She spent the morning opening and closing her free hand. She watched her fist clench and then relax. She could see it happening, but she couldn't feel it. After a while, she would shift her load and work the other hand. By noon the air was warm enough that her hands began to thaw.

Rosmerta thought she felt the tingling again, or maybe she just imagined it. Then her hands went from pale to bright red. At first, she took this as a hopeful sign—then the pain hit. She tried to keep flexing. Tears were running down her cheeks. *Just ignore the pain*, she told herself, while clenching her teeth in agony. She let out a squeak just loud enough that Emma heard her.

"You're in pain. I'll take Megerdich," Emma said.

"No," said Rosmerta. "I can do it."

"I know you can, sweetie. But you need to take care of your hands. Give Megerdich to me, and rub your hands together.

Rosmerta was embarrassed by all the fuss. She could have managed. She started rubbing her hands together. At least Boghos wasn't here to see this. She didn't want him thinking she wasn't carrying her share of the load.

Rosmerta was still trying to warm her hands as they approached the next campsite. Boghos ran up to them, saying, "This way, hurry."

"Come on, Boghos," said Emma, panting. "We're exhausted. Can't we just stop here?"

"It's not far. Just a few more feet." His voice was almost sparkling with enthusiasm.

Reluctantly, the women followed him to a small tent sitting by a stream.

"What do you think?" he asked. "I set it up myself."

"Where did you…" Rosmerta stopped herself. The night had been cold. Undoubtedly some people didn't survive. She decided she didn't want to know where Boghos got the tent. It was enough that they had somewhere to stay warm for the night.

There was no food. They all laid down in the small tent and tried to sleep. The pain in Rosmerta's hands was unbearable. Emma tried to comfort her, but it was no use. Rosmerta shivered and moaned her way through the night. As painful as it was, the tent trapped just enough body warmth that her hands mostly recovered by morning.

The sun rose too early and Rosmerta emerged from their refuge to find a layer of snow covering everything. The group quickly rolled up the tent and the caravan was on its way again. The day warmed quickly, melting the snow and revealing a muddy path through the woods.

After several days in the mountains, many more people were left behind, and the only food were the berries and roots they could find by the side of the well-worn trail.

One morning, while traversing an especially rocky area, Shushawn twisted her ankle badly. Even with a noticeable limp, she insisted on taking her turn carrying Megerdich. They were walking along a narrow ledge, Shushawn up front, with Rosmerta behind her, followed by Emma. Boghos was off on his own again. They had gotten used to that. The only consolation was that they seemed to be descending now, and everyone was relieved that the mountains would soon be behind them.

They came to the top of a tall rock cliff. Far below, they observed a field covered in dead bodies. In a sudden flash of comprehension, Rosmerta knew where they were. This was the second killing field. At the far end, she could make out the clump of trees where Adelina had given birth.

"We're back," said Emma, her voice breaking in despair. "We haven't gone anywhere."

Shushawn stopped and glanced back at Rosmerta. Her eyes were pleading. She stared down at the outcropping of rocks below. "May God have mercy on my soul," she said, just loud enough for Rosmerta to hear. She closed her eyes, held Megerdich tight to her chest, and stepped over the edge.

"No!" cried Rosmerta. It was too late. Shushawn fell to the base of the cliff and lay motionless. Baby Megerdich was underneath her. There was nothing Rosmerta and Emma could do but continue on. Sure enough, they descended to the same trail they had traveled only a few days earlier. This time, instead of going into the mountains, they traveled through the valley.

It helped that the lowlands stayed warmer at night. Even without the extreme cold, rest was hard to come by. Of the Bedrosians, only Emma, Boghos, and Rosmerta were left. The tent was plenty large enough. Emma was sobbing in the corner. Rosmerta lay awake listening.

Only Boghos managed to fall asleep. As soon as he was out, he woke with a start. His eyes popped open as he let out a blood curdling shriek. "Stay here," he yelled, jumping up and running out of the tent to confront the attacking soldiers. He turned to his left, then his right. He spun all the way around. "How dare you!" he screamed.

A woman came out of a nearby tent. "What is it? What's going on?"

"The Soldiers," said Boghos. "They're back."

The woman stood up straight and looked around. "There are no soldiers."

More heads popped out their tents.

Rosmerta looked out. "What is it Boghos?"

"It's nothing," someone said. "Go back to bed."

Boghos looked bewildered. Rosmerta went to him and tried to lead him back into the tent.

"But they're coming."

"No one is coming Boghos. There is no one out there. Come on, get back in the tent."

By the time everyone settled down, it was time to get up and prepare for another march.

Erzincan

The caravan was led through a narrow valley. After several days, the valley opened to expose a small town. Erzincan sat in a lush green basin, surrounded by snow-capped mountains. They had been so close to this town when they first climbed into the mountains. The whole mountain episode had been orchestrated for the sole purpose of killing people.

The procession passed through the center of town to a small square covered in the improvised tents of another Armenian group. Boghos was near the front of the caravan. He found a gap between two tents and had started setting up for the night when Emma and Rosmerta found him. As usual, Rosmerta took the jug and went looking for water.

A crowd was gathered around a well on the north side of the square. Rosmerta approached to see what was happening.

"Please Mama, water," pleaded a little girl.

"Soon," said her mother.

"What's wrong?" asked Rosmerta. "Why can't you get water?"

"The guards won't let anyone near the well unless they pay. I don't have any money. Do you?"

"No," replied Rosmerta, realizing the horrible truth. Shushawn, as the matriarch of the group, had all the money, and her body was twenty miles back on the trail. Rosmerta wandered around town for a while. She saw some deportees buying food and clothing, complaining about the ridiculous prices they had to pay. At least they were getting what they needed. Rosmerta also realized that the buyers were far

97

outnumbered by people like her who had no money and nothing to eat. Money talked in Erzincan, and she had none.

Rosmerta patted her right hip. *I have the comb*, she reminded herself. But what was she to do with it? Could she trade it for food? Should she try to sell it? Who would buy it? How much was it worth? She had to talk with Boghos. He seemed to know how to get things done.

She returned to camp to find Emma and Boghos munching on a loaf of bread. "Where did you get that?"

"He stole it," said Emma. "Here." She handed a piece to Rosmerta.

"We need money," Rosmerta said between bites.

"I know," said Boghos. "We'll get some later. At least we have food for tonight."

He was right. They were okay tonight. Her comb would remain her secret for now.

A rumor spread throughout the camp that they were to be on the move again in the morning. Erzincan was a small town and could not handle all these refugees. The people who traveled from Gumushkhane complained that they were here first and the group from Bayburt would have to find their own place. Those from Bayburt insisted that they needed rest after their long march and that those from Gumushkhane were well rested and should leave Erzincan to them. A fight nearly broke out between the two factions, when a group of Muslim men came storming into the tent city.

At first, the Armenians thought they were soldiers coming to break up the fight. It wasn't long before they knew the truth. These men were looking for women. Rosmerta watched in horror as a man picked up a young girl from a neighboring tent and carried her away. The girl's mother ran after her. The kidnapper sliced her face open with his sword. The woman kept stumbling forward, flailing at the air. With blood in her eyes, she couldn't see and fell. The man disappeared with her daughter.

Other men were taking their prizes as well. Some carried girls off and others simply raped them in their tents and left them as so much waste. Rosmerta and Emma hurried into the tent while Boghos stood guard at the entrance. Several men studied him threateningly. Boghos stood firm. Although he was small, he was male. There were very few males left in the group. While Boghos probably couldn't put up much of a fight, it was easier for the marauders to leave him alone and find another target. Eventually all the men got what they came for—a wife or some shorter-term pleasure—and they left the camp. Boghos slipped back into the tent and joined the women. "They're gone," he said.

Rosmerta reached up to hug Boghos. They embraced for a long time. "I was so scared," she said.

"So was I," he said. "But they're gone now."

Rosmerta glanced at Emma, who was staring into space, totally non-responsive. She looked back at Boghos, tears appearing in her eyes.

He sat beside Rosmerta, wrapping his arm around her shoulders and pulling her towards him. Her head resting on Boghos' shoulder, Rosmerta wept.

Emma's trance was broken. She watched the young couple, opened her mouth to speak, then thought better of it. She rolled over to face the side of the tent.

After a while, Boghos asked, "Do you remember the Trndez festival before Aghavni was married?"

Rosmerta shook her head.

"I sure do. That's the night I was told we were betrothed. Aghavni brought the fire to us for Shushawn. When people started jumping over the fire in celebration of their coming wedding, I wanted to join them. My father said I was too young. He pointed at you and said, 'See Rosmerta over there? She's not jumping either. In a few years, you two can jump the fire together.' Just then, you ran past us and jumped. I looked at my father and he just shrugged. So, I jumped too. After that, I decided that having you as my wife would be okay."

Rosmerta looked up at Boghos and pulled him closer.

He laid his head on hers. She was no longer crying.

To Sivas and Beyond

The next morning, the gendarmes rounded up the entire Armenian camp, both the Gumushkhane and Bayburt factions, and escorted them out of town. They traveled along the western branch of the Euphrates River towards Sivas.

Boghos, Emma, and Rosmerta stayed together—there was strength in numbers. They avoided the end of the procession where impatient gendarmes culled the weak. They stayed far enough behind the leaders that they hoped they could see traps before they were sprung.

The terrain was difficult at first. There were many hills, but nothing like the mountains they had passed through on the way to Erzincan. The hills got smaller as they progressed until the terrain was almost flat. They covered fifteen to twenty miles each day. Some days they were wet. Some days they were hot. They were cold every night. Food was always difficult, but early summer was a decent time for finding bugs, and they usually managed to scrounge something along the way. With no more surprise attacks by the Special Forces, the trip was relatively uneventful, though every day the camp was a little smaller. It seemed that the impatient gendarmes were staying busy.

It took eight days to reach Sivas. By the time they got there, the caravan's population had been cut in half. Rosmerta realized that the demographics of this group were very different from the original population of their hometowns. There were no elderly people, and it was rare to see anyone who was too young to manage the trip by themselves. Those who remained were thin. Their clothes were little more than dirty rags hanging off skin-covered skeletons.

Rosmerta was hungry. She tried to concentrate on anything else. All she could think about was food. She thought about the yogurt she made back in Bayburt. She thought about sitting around the fire at night munching on almonds and pistachios. She remembered summer celebrations with bright flavorful dishes accented with fresh herbs of cilantro, parsley, dill, and mint. She reminisced about sitting in the courtyard with her father eating squash seeds and spitting out the shells. She thought about winter meals with dried figs and dates, prunes and raisins, and of course apricots. She thought about winter festivals with their soul satisfying meals of boiled lamb, bulgur pilaf, and thin round bread. She thought about Shushawn cooking all day, filling the house with smells of cinnamon and cloves, nutmeg, and allspice. There were stews flavored with rose water and spicy dishes with peppers, paprika, and fenugreek. Shushawn had promised to teach Rosmerta how to make chaimen paste. Who would teach her now? Would she ever taste anything as amazing as that again?

Rosmerta was still thinking about food as they approached Sivas. There was a slight rise in the trail. She didn't see it and stumbled, scraping the palms of her hands as she landed face first in the dirt. Her chin was bleeding. Boghos rushed to help her up. "Are you okay, Rose?"

"Yeah, I'm fine." She brushed the dirt off her hands and looked around for the bundle of blankets she had dropped. Embarrassed, she gathered up her things and continued down the path.

Boghos walked beside her. "You know, I don't remember anyone else in your family named Rosmerta. Where did your name come from?"

"My mother. She died bringing me into the world. My father named me after her."

"What do you know about her?" Boghos asked.

"Almost nothing. My father talked about Anoush, his first wife, all the time. He barely ever talked about my mother."

"What about your brothers? Didn't they tell you anything?"

"Aghavni told me she had curly hair like mine, and green eyes. I don't think Hagop or Papken were old enough to remember much." Rosmerta's voice was trembling. Reminiscing about her family brought back many memories of events she would rather forget.

They walked in silence until they entered a camp outside Sivas housing groups from all over Northern Anatolia. Each group had a designated area within the camp. To add insult to the already overwhelming injury of the deportation, the area where Rosmerta and her remaining family would stay was referred to as the Gumushkhane section.

They set up, and Boghos left to find food. It seemed to be a particular talent of his.

"I'll get the water tonight. You stay and get a fire started," said Emma.

"Why do I have to stay at the camp? It's my job to get water," Rosmerta protested.

"You're injured," Emma said, gesturing to the gash on Rosmerta's chin. "You need to rest. Just get a fire going. We'll be back soon."

Rosmerta had a flame going when she saw a group of young men coming into the Gumushkhane section. They were Muslim men from Sivas, a few years shy of being old enough to join the Turkish Army. Bored, they had come to check out the new arrivals. Rosmerta thought about slipping into the tent to hide but saw that the men were checking the tents. There were five of them. The leader was carrying a sword. He approached Rosmerta. "No need for you to worry dear, we're looking for your men. You don't know where we might find them, do you?"

"No," Rosmerta lied. As she said it, she saw an Armenian boy, no older than thirteen, walking towards them.

"Leave her alone," the boy said.

"You'll do nicely," said the leader, nodding to his men. Two of them stepped up and grabbed the boy. "And I lied about you," he said to Rosmerta. The other two men grabbed her and dragged her away from the camp. Rosmerta knew no one would follow them. Anyone who saw her being taken would be relieved that it was her and not them. She knew the feeling well.

The leader was tall and muscular with broad shoulders and a wide chin. His beard was thin but neatly trimmed. In Bayburt, Rosmerta might have considered him handsome. Here, after all the miles, all the death, and especially the constant hunger, such things didn't even occur to her. "We'll take care of him first," he said.

"What do we do with the girl?"

"Tie her legs together, and tie her hands behind her back."

The young men wrapped a rope around Rosmerta's knees.

"Not like that. Tie her ankles together."

"Come on Fedime. If you're so smart, do it yourself."

"Just get it done, then leave her sitting up, leaning on that rock. I want her to see what we do to infidel men."

When Rosmerta was constrained, the men turned their attention to the young boy. They grabbed him and pushed him to the ground. Two men held down his arms while the other two had his legs. He flailed around for a while, but soon tired. Realizing the futility of his situation, he lay still on his back. Fedime knelt with his knees on either side of the boy's head. He put one hand on the boy's forehead and held his sword high in the other hand. He started to chant in Arabic, though he had been speaking to his friends in Turkish.

A thought flashed in Rosmerta's mind—this is what Boghos said happened to him in the house on the outskirts of Bayburt. This time, there was no chance of Muhammad Kasaba stopping the proceedings.

The chanting continued for a while, then Fedime Tarik lowered his sword to the boy's throat. Fedime raised his eyes to heaven, then returned his attention to the boy, who jerked his head away. Fedime pushed hard on the knife. The blade cut through the boy's jugular vein and half way through his windpipe. Blood gushed out, pooling around his head. There was a wheezing sound as air escaped through the hole in his neck.

Fedime sliced across the boy's throat again, cutting all the way to his vertebrae. His body lay still while his head thrashed back and forth. A final push, and the boy's head was completely severed from his body. Fedime grabbed it by the hair and stood holding it aloft in triumph.

Rosmerta thought she was going to throw up. She shut her eyes to avoid the scene. The image of the knife cutting into the boy's neck would not leave her. She was glad to be sitting down. Surely, she would have passed out if she had been standing.

To Rosmerta, the greatest shock was that none of this actually surprised her. She had seen so much death and so much senseless violence that while this certainly didn't seem normal, neither did it seem extraordinary.

After a few prayers, Fedime Tarik walked over to Rosmerta. He grabbed the rope holding her ankles together and pulled hard. The back of her head slammed against the rock, then dragged on the ground until she lay straight out on her back. Her vision went out of focus and she blinked, trying to get it back. Her arms were twisted behind her and pinned in place. She tried to raise her upper body to release her arms but Fedime pushed her back down.

Fedime untied the rope binding Rosmerta's legs and lifted her dress. "What do we have here?" he said as he reached for a red satchel. He opened the silk package to find the beautiful silver hair comb. "Oh, this is very nice. My mother will like this." He tossed the comb to one of his friends and pulled down Rosmerta's underwear. She flailed about, trying to throw him off. Fedime lay on top of her, grabbing her by the throat and squeezing hard. "Give me a knife," he said. One of the other boys stepped forward holding a knife out to Fedime. Rosmerta froze. "That's better. Now don't make me hurt you."

Rosmerta felt Fedime enter her. The pain was intense. She couldn't move. The deeper he went, the more revolting he was to Rosmerta. She began to feel light-headed and nauseated. After a while, her stomach settled down. Then she didn't feel anything. She knew what was happening to her, but it was as if it was happening to someone else's body. She was a distant observer. The whole thing was still outrageous and disturbing, yet somehow unreal.

When Fedime Tarik finished, the other four took their turns in succession. Rosmerta watched it all from a distance. When the last one was done, the young men disappeared and left her lying on the ground. She began to shake.

The slack expression on her face was replaced by a tense grimace. Tears began to flow. She tried to roll over. As soon as she moved, pain from her left shoulder tore through her entire body. For the first time since the ordeal began, Rosmerta made a noise. It was a piercing, shrill, unnerving shriek powered by every sinew of her being. Her entire body tensed as she pushed every last ounce of energy she had left into a noise that gave voice to her pain, and outrage, and fear, and panic, expressing feelings that until this moment she didn't even know existed. She felt as if she were screaming out all the pain her people had suffered.

When the scream ended, Rosmerta lay still. Even the shaking was gone. She rolled over onto her stomach then rose to her knees. She could tell that something was very wrong with her left shoulder. She tried to release her hands from their bindings, but every movement sent a sharp pain radiating down her arm. She swung her foot forward and tried to stand. She fell on her first attempt. Balancing without arms is difficult. More careful the second time, she succeeded.

Boghos and Emma returned to the tent and found Rosmerta was gone. The fire was still going. When one of their neighbors told them that Rosmerta and the other boy were taken by a group of Muslims from town, Boghos and Emma were concerned but also confused. "The other boy?" Obviously the lady had it wrong. There was no other boy. She must have misread what was happening. It was understandable. Everyone was a little paranoid these days. Emma stayed at the tent in case Rosmerta returned, while Boghos went out to look for her.

When Rosmerta reached the edge of the camp, she stopped. She was embarrassed to be seen tied up like an animal. She stood there, undecided what to do. She recalled returning to her brother's wedding celebration after being accosted by Ahmet. She had feared that her entire family would know what she had done, even though she hadn't actually done anything. Now, disgraced and bound, there was no way to enter the camp without everyone knowing. Yes, this was much worse. But what choice did she have?

Rosmerta raised her head in defiance and walked purposefully into the camp. Most people ignored her. Some people stared. She passed several rows of tents before someone finally came to her aid. "Oh my!" exclaimed a short woman with a gentle voice. "I have a knife. We'll get this off you."

"Were you raped?" the woman asked. Rosmerta nodded. A woman in a neighboring tent glared at her in shock and disgust and went back into her tent.

"Oh, don't mind her," said the gentle voice. "Now stay still." The woman cut the rope, and Rosmerta's left arm dropped to her side. She screamed and grabbed her left shoulder. The gentle woman looked on in alarm.

Hearing Rosmerta's cry, Boghos came running. She put up her right arm to stop him before he tried to embrace her. It was too late. He crushed her in his arms. She let out another shriek. Boghos stepped back, examining her. "Can you move it?" he asked, nodding to her left arm. Rosmerta shook her head.

She flinched and looked away when Boghos reached for her shoulder. "It's dislocated," he said, confirming her fear. "We'll have to reset it. That's going to hurt."

Rosmerta nodded. She was crying now. Boghos rested one hand on her shoulder and pulled down on her arm with the other. She let out a sharp gasp. The shoulder was still dislocated. Boghos pulled again. It wasn't going to work.

"She's fainting," announced the short woman. Rosmerta's eyes had a vacant look and the color had left her face. Boghos caught her as she fell back into his arms. He set her on the ground.

"That's okay, I'll hold her and you pull."

The woman got behind Rosmerta and held her, while Boghos grabbed her arm with both hands and pulled again. The shoulder joint felt loose, but the arm did not reset. With one foot on each side of her arm, Boghos pulled again. All he accomplished was bringing Rosmerta and the woman towards him. Then he saw it. "Let her down," said Boghos. He put his left foot into Rosmerta's armpit, grabbed her arm, and pulled with all his might. There was a loud *click* and her arm went back into its socket.

Rosmerta woke with a start, looked at Boghos, and passed out again. A couple minutes later, she came to. The sharp pain was gone, replaced by a general soreness. She was able to move her arm, but it felt better if she didn't. Boghos helped her to her feet and led her back to their tent.

"What happened to you?" Emma exclaimed when they returned.

"Nothing," Rosmerta grumbled as she moved to the back of the tent.

"You're hurt! Where have you been?"

"It's nothing," Rosmerta insisted. "Leave me alone." She covered her face and turned away.

Boghos reached out to put his arm around her.

Rosmerta slapped him away. "Leave – me – alone!" she hissed.

Boghos recoiled in shock and exited the tent.

Rosmerta saw little of Boghos over the next few days. She spent most of her time in the tent recuperating. Physically, she was feeling better every day. However, as much as she tried, she couldn't keep herself from reliving the horrors in her mind—the brutal murder of the young boy, the pain of being raped, and the shame. She hadn't fought back at all. She did nothing. She just let it happen.

And there was the fear—what if she was pregnant by one of those foul beasts? How long would it be before she would know? What would Emma think? How would Boghos react? He must realize that she had been raped. He didn't seem to fault her for that. Or did he? Where was he? He had been avoiding her. But that's because she yelled at him, right? Not because he hated her. Or maybe he did. She wasn't sure she liked herself. But that short woman didn't judge her. And Rosmerta had never thanked her. How could she not thank the woman who saved her?

She walked over to the section of the camp where she had met her and found that it was empty. Its former inhabitants were off on another pointless march. Rosmerta would never know the woman's name.

A few more days passed, and the gendarmes came to collect another group. Rosmerta, Emma, and Boghos were back on the trail to nowhere.

Boghos carried the tent, while Emma carried their remaining possessions—a small knife, the water jug, and a loaf of bread Boghos managed to scrounge up. Rosmerta's arm was in a sling made from a strip of canvas cut from the edge of the tent. With only one working arm, she was not carrying anything. It was July, and the temperature climbed to over 100 degrees most days. On the third day, Boghos left the tent behind. The bread was long gone.

Shuffling along the dry dirt path, a cloud of dust rose behind them. Rosmerta tried to stay focused on keeping her feet moving. No matter how hard she concentrated, her mind wandered. She thought back to her life in Bayburt. It seemed so long ago. She thought of her father. Megerdich had been so decent and so kind to everyone. How could they shoot him?

If they had seen him sending the recently engaged young men out to gather wood for the Trndez bonfire, they would have known what kind of a man he was. Even in his old age, Megerdich always orchestrated the town's Trndez festivities. On his instructions, the young men would stack wood in a pile on the church grounds. The pile was set alight on the night of February thirteenth. After the priest blessed the fire, the men would grab a piece of wood from the burning pile and run to the house of their intended, where another fire was lit with the flame. Before long, the whole town was ablaze with bonfires. Rosmerta remembered the scene fondly because, by the time the fires were lit along the streets of Bayburt, her father had returned home, and she would be sitting with him watching the dancing flames. It was wonderful.

The night had great significance for the whole village. Engaged couples could not see each other from the time of their engagement until the day of their wedding, except during the Trndez rituals. And Candlemas Day itself—the day after the fires—was the last day couples could get married until after Easter. There were always many weddings then. And weddings meant parties and food.

Food again. Every sequence of thoughts led to food. It was customary to eat porridge on Trndez. Rosmerta learned how to make it at the last festival. As she stood over the fire stirring the wheat and water mixture, Shushawn had slapped her hand, saying, "Never stir porridge. It is bad luck."

Rosmerta shook her head. It wasn't a happy memory. It didn't matter—porridge wasn't the best part of Trndez anyway. That distinction went to *aghandz*, a fabulous crunchy snack of salty roasted grains with seeds and nuts.

Rosmerta brought herself back to reality. Walking was as easy as it could be. Nourishment came in the form of grass picked from the side of the trail. Thirst was the biggest problem, and the heat caused many people to give up. After five days, the party reached another camp outside the town of Malatya. It was much dryer than where they came from.

Everyone was covered in dirt. It coated their faces, infused their hair, and saturated all their clothing.

The camp was filthy too. It was filled with emaciated, desperate occupants. Food was almost impossible to find, and many people starved to death. The camp was infested with lice. They were in the Malatya camp for less than a week. For the first time since the deportation, they were glad to move on.

But the next leg of their journey was sheer torture. The convoy moved in and out of the mountains several times. The lice were relentless. Rosmerta wiped them out of her eyes and spit them out of her mouth. She couldn't get away from them.

There were bodies all along the road. Most of them were naked. Any clothing they had was taken by someone soon after they dropped. The hot sun burned the bodies to an almost unrecognizable charcoal black. At one point they passed a group of six smooth round rocks lying on the ground in the shape of a cross. The bloated body next to it looked like a grotesque giant pomegranate with arms, legs, and a head. Rosmerta averted her eyes and moved along.

That same day, Emma started scratching at her arms. Sores appeared there after a couple more days. The lesions spread over her arms and face. The itching was intense. The next day, they were walking across a desolate landscape and saw another bloated body by the roadside. When they reached it, they saw six rocks placed carefully on the ground in the shape of a cross. They were walking in circles.

When they passed the rock cross formation the third time, the grotesque form next to it was crawling with worms. By now, Emma's scabies covered her entire body. The site of the same miserable location was too much. Emma collapsed beside the cross and just stopped.

Rosmerta glanced back to see the end of the procession closing in on them. "Emma, come on. We have to go."

Emma raised her head slightly but did not look at Rosmerta. She opened her mouth as if to speak, then lowered her head without saying anything.

"Emma!" Rosmerta screamed. She was in a total panic now. "Emma, we have to go." She tried to lift her, but she couldn't do it. "Emma! Get up!"

There was no response. Emma slumped there, her breathing becoming increasingly shallow. She was done. The trailing gendarme reached them.

"Emma, I'm sorry. I have to go." Rosmerta stood tall and scurried on past a few people in order to get away from the gendarme, leaving Emma in the middle of the road.

Three weeks after leaving Malatya, they reached their next temporary settlement. Urfa was a much larger town than the last couple they had visited. The camp was isolated—there was no chance to interact with the town itself. There was a small pond at the edge of the camp. Actually, it wasn't much more than a large puddle. A group of soldiers was keeping anyone from getting to it. When someone couldn't stand it any longer and lunged forward for a drink, one of the soldiers would hit them with the butt of his rifle. One particularly aggressive woman kept charging forward. Even with blood pouring from her head, she refused to relent. A bayonet to the gut ended her struggle.

One little boy was pleading with his mother. "Thirsty, Mama. Please, Mama."

"Not now, you must be patient."

"Why, Mama?"

"God is working in ways we do not know, but nonetheless working. We must take pleasure in suffering for Christ's sake."

Rosmerta didn't think the woman was talking to her son anymore. Maybe she was trying to convince herself to keep going. Maybe she was praying. All Rosmerta knew for sure was that staying around this pond wasn't going to get her anywhere. She moved on.

She found Boghos sitting by himself, his eyes greedily fixed on the pitcher in her hand. "It's empty," she said. "They won't let us have water. Did you find anything?"

"No." He looked away in shame.

His magic was fading. There was no food. "What are we supposed to do?" Rosmerta asked.

"Not much we can do. We'll have to wait and try again later."

"Do you remember that year they built the well in Bayburt?"

"How could I forget? We had more visitors that summer than we ever had before. Your father spent as much time with us as he did with you."

"That was the year my father first let me go into town with him. He said that when I got older, I wouldn't be able to leave the house and he wanted me to see Bayburt before it was too late."

"My sisters never went into town," said Boghos. "I don't think they ever got beyond our courtyard—until they left, that is. Now I don't know where they are. I'm glad they got away. It's just that I miss them so much. I hope they're okay, but I have no way to know."

"Where were they going?"

"I don't know. Sivas, I think. I don't think they were planning on staying there."

"We just left Sivas."

"Don't you think I know that? I tried to get out of the camp to look for them. I couldn't get past the guards."

"The Muslim boys from town didn't have any problem coming and going at will."

Boghos gave her a look of pity.

Rosmerta didn't know what to say. They sat in silence for a long time.

After nightfall, they went back to the pond to find that the soldiers were gone. They drank their fill, returned to their patch of earth, and fell asleep. They awoke to find that someone had stolen their water jug. Now they truly had nothing.

The evacuation order came a few days later. Boghos and Rosmerta were on the march again. The Syrian Desert is a barren place. The days when Rosmerta could step off the trail and eat the grass seemed like a dream. There was nothing to eat here. Some people resorted to picking barley seeds out of animal dung. The heat was furious, reaching 120 degrees at midday.

The only advantage the desert offered was that breaks came more frequently. This was not out of any concern for the Armenians. Rather, the gendarmes' horses were struggling with the heat.

One day, the gendarmes climbed back onto their horses after a break and road quickly away from the refugees. Everyone braced themselves for the attack they were sure was coming. Instead, another group of gendarmes arrived to replace the first. This band was riding camels. There would be no more frequent stops.

It would have been bad enough if fewer breaks had been the worst of it, but this group of gendarmes was especially brutal. When the sun first lit the camp the next morning and the refugees fell into line, they were given an unusual order.

"Take off your clothes and put them in a pile over here," said one of the gendarmes from high on his camel. No one moved. "You," he said pointing to a young girl near him. "Take them off." She looked around then back at the gendarme. He raised his gun. She pulled her dingy shift over her head. She stood there in front of everyone in only her underwear. "Those too," he said. She did as she was told. "Come on now—all of you." The entire camp stripped naked.

Rosmerta was horrified by her own body. Not that she was embarrassed to be naked in front of everyone—any sense of modesty had been lost a long way back on the trail. She had known she was getting thin, but this was the first time she had really examined herself. She could see all her ribs. Her hip bones jutted up and out as if they were trying to escape her skin. Her legs were long thin bones with bulbous knee joints. Boghos was every bit as emaciated as she was. His face, which she had been looking at the whole trip, appeared caved in now that she saw it in the context of his entire body. His cheeks and temples were hollow. His eyes were sunken deep into his head. His collar bones and shoulder blades were razor sharp. She checked—yes, hers were the same. She was sure she could see Boghos' spine through his stomach. It occurred to Rosmerta that if she had seen Boghos naked a few short months ago, she would have found it exciting. Now it was just pitiful. From the look on his face, it appeared that Boghos felt the same way about her.

The day's march was long, and the sun had unfettered access to every inch of the travelers' skin. By noon, they knew they were being burned. There was no way to avoid it. That night, the pain began to emerge as if it had been hiding just under the surface all along. Rosmerta's skin was tight and dry. Every time she adjusted her position, she felt it.

In the morning, she was hot and nauseated. Her skin was peeling off her body in large sheets. This, of course, exposed a new, tender layer to the merciless sun.

At about noon, the party reached the Euphrates River at Jerablus. They would have to make a crossing. The gendarmes found a bridge. They split the Armenians into two groups. The gendarmes and a group that included Boghos walked across the bridge. The other travelers, including Rosmerta, would have to ford the river.

The first group of Armenians was not allowed to even drink the water. The second had to pull themselves through it. Rosmerta reached the edge of the river and dipped her foot in. It was cold. She reached down and took a drink. She could feel the water sliding down her throat and through the center of her chest. When the cold water reached bottom, Rosmerta could feel her stomach contract.

She moved further into the fast-moving river. She saw people climbing out on the other side. She went in up to her knees, then had to step down until her legs disappeared. Her muscles tensed to the point where she wasn't sure she could move. She forced herself to take a step. Her foot slipped, and she was entirely submerged. She struggled to the surface. The river was sweeping her away. She wasn't alone. Several others were floating down river with her. Rosmerta fought to keep her head above water. Her leg smashed into a rock, swinging her body around. She was surfing headfirst down the river. She reached for another rock and managed to stop. She thrashed and kicked her way to the west bank and dragged herself out of the river. There, she collapsed from exhaustion and passed out.

Throwing Stones

Umar and Wasim had grown up together. While they were best friends, there was always a certain tension in their friendship. They had been told not to go near the river many times, but it was where they always played. Besides, what were a few dead bodies?

Okay, it was more than a few. Corpses had been floating down the river for several months. They used to come in pairs—two bodies tied together drifting past Jerablus. Occasionally, there would be four bodies rafted together. Four was too many. They often got caught on things in the river and sat there rotting. The smell was horrible. Recently, there had been many single bodies floating down the river. Those were ideal—they were small enough targets to make it a challenge and they never got hung up on anything for long.

"Wow, there are a lot of them today," said Umar as he picked a small, round stone and threw it at a corpse passing by below.

"Oh, you can't hit anything," Wasim chided. "Let me show you how it's done." He threw his stone and hit a pair of bodies coming behind the one Umar had missed. It struck one of the pair in the back.

"Yeah," said Umar, "but that was a double. Anyone can hit those."

"Well, watch this then," said Wasim as he wound up and threw again. This time he hit a single body as it whooshed by. He watched as it rushed downstream. "Hey, look," he said, "over there."

"I see it." Umar wound up again, aiming for a body lying on the bank. He missed again.

"You are terrible. That one isn't even moving. Wasim threw a stone and hit its leg. The leg jerked forward. "Hey, that one's alive."

Umar and Wasim ran down the embankment and along the river to the body that wasn't dead. It was a girl. She shook her head and rubbed her leg. She rolled over into a sitting position facing the river.

"Careful Umar, you don't know what she's up to."

"She's lying naked beside a river. How much trouble can she be?"

"She's Armenian. My father says that Armenians are filthy, evil beasts, filled with hatred and wicked intentions."

"I know what your father says," interrupted Umar. He stopped himself from telling Wasim what he really thought of his family's world view.

The Armenian girl looked scared. Her matted hair made it clear she had been in the river. The fact that it was completely dry indicated that she must have come out of the water some time ago. The girl pulled her knees up to her chest and wrapped her arms around her legs. She opened and closed her mouth.

"She's trying to speak," said Umar. He leaned down next to the girl and strained to listen. He couldn't make it out. "I'm Umar," he said. "We want to help you."

"What?" Wasim said. "We're going to take her home and feed her, I guess. Like a family pet or something. If an

Armenian shows up at my house, my father will kill her. And if I bring her there, he'll kill me too."

"We're not taking her to your house. I'm taking her to mine, and if you don't want to help, then leave."

"Maybe I will. Besides, look at her. She looks terrible. She's beyond thin—she's almost transparent. She'll be dead soon, no matter what you do."

The Armenian girl jerked her head towards Wasim and stared at him with a look of disdain.

"See," said Wasim, "she even looks evil. I think she's putting a curse on me or something."

"You're upset because even Armenian girls don't like you. Now either help me or go."

"Umar, look at her. She's almost dead. And the way she's looking at me, she hates me."

"Of course she hates you. You keep saying she's going to die. That's not going to happen. I'll take her home and we'll make her better. My father won't let another person die if he can help it, even if she is Armenian."

A New Home

Rosmerta woke up to the noise of banging pots and pans. She was in a small room lying on a straw mat on a wooden floor, covered with a light blanket. She couldn't remember how she got here. She felt pretty good. She pulled the blanket down to see that she was wearing a clean white shift. Her body was clean too. Even her hair felt soft and smooth. She heard another clang from outside her room. Where was she?

The door opened, and a tall, well-dressed woman came in. "You're awake."

"Where am I?" Rosmerta tried to ask. It came out as a low gravelly croak.

"Shh, save your voice. It will be a while before you can speak. Wait here, I'll get you something to drink."

The elegant woman turned and left. Rosmerta scanned the room. She seemed to be hidden away in an interior space with no windows and only one door. The woman returned with a cup of sweet tea. At first she tried to get Rosmerta to drink it, but she couldn't swallow. With no other option, the woman soaked a rag with the tea and let Rosmerta suck on it. It soothed her dry mouth, and she could feel it as it slid down her parched throat. After a second helping, Rosmerta fell back to sleep.

When she woke again, there was a cup of tea waiting for her. She pulled herself to a sitting position and drank it quickly.

The tall woman returned with a piece of bread and more tea. Rosmerta's voice was still rough, but comprehensible. "Where am I?"

"You are in Jarablus."

"Jarablus, where's that?" Rosmerta coughed. Her throat was still dry.

"Jarablus is in the Aleppo Vilayet."

"I'm still in the Ottoman Empire?"

"Yes, in the Syrian Provinces."

"Whose house is this?"

"You are in the home of Rasim Sengor."

"Are you his wife?"

"No," laughed the woman. "I am Amtullah. I am a servant to the Sengors. Sir Rasim is married to Madam Zayna."

"How did I get here?"

Amtullah explained to Rosmerta how the Sengors' son Umar had found her by the river and brought her to the house. Once she started talking, Amtullah became very informative. In addition to Umar, the Sengors had an older son who died in the Balkan wars. There was also a daughter who had died young, but Amtullah seemed not to want to talk about that.

Over the next few weeks, Rosmerta regained her strength. At first, she didn't eat much. Eventually her appetite returned. Her burned skin took the longest to heal, the pain subsiding over time.

Rasim Sengor was a small man with a big heart. He was kind to Rosmerta and asked many questions about her family and her journey to Jerablus. When she was strong enough, he took her out to the garden where they would sit and watch the birds playing in the fruit trees.

Rasim taught Rosmerta how to distinguish a Syrian woodpecker from a great spotted woodpecker by the length of their beaks. He pointed out the difference between the twitter of a desert lark and the high-pitched tweet of the Menetries's warbler.

One day, Rasim and Rosmerta were practicing bird calls, when he squatted in front of her and hopped around with his arms outstretched and pointed down and behind him like wings. He flapped his arms and raised his head while mimicking the melodic song of the beautiful ortalon.

Rosmerta burst out laughing. It was the first time she could remember laughing since she left Bayburt.

Rasim stopped his song and looked at Rosmerta with kind but distant eyes. He sank back and sat on the ground in front of her. "You remind me of my daughter Neyla. She had an amazing laugh, too."

It was the first time Rosmerta had heard the girl's name. "What happened to your Neyla? How did she die?"

"It was years ago," Rasim's voice was sad, but he was still smiling. "She was a happy child. She ran everywhere. You couldn't slow her down. She laughed at everything. So joyful. She didn't like birds though. When she was very young, she was watching a hawk fly slow, sweeping circles above the garden. It pooped on her head. She never forgave the bird community for that. I like that you like birds, Rosmerta. I enjoy our time in the garden."

"I do too," Rosmerta said.

"When Neyla was about your age, she got sick," Rasim continued, his smile fading. "It happened quickly. One day she was fine. The next morning, she couldn't get out of bed. The doctors were no help. They had no idea what it was. 'Some virus' is all they could come up with. Whatever it was, it killed over a hundred people in Jerablus that year." Rasim looked up at Rosmerta. "But now we have you," he said as the smile returned to his face.

Rosmerta wasn't sure how to interpret this. Was she merely a pale imitation of the daughter he had lost? Some sort of ghost giving him a few good memories? *No*, she thought. They had the garden and the birds. Even so, Rosmerta was never sure of her relationship with Rasim after that. Nevertheless, she kept going to the garden and enjoying the birds with him.

The warblers were Rosmerta's favorite. A pair had built a nest in the scrubby thickets of the tamarisk bushes. She would sit for hours watching the pair return over and over with food for their chicks. Even before they were big enough to see, Rosmerta could hear them chirping. After a couple weeks, their heads could be seen peeking up above the sides of the nest. One day when Rosmerta passed the shrub, two birds swooped out, almost hitting the ground before flying off. She had just enough time to look up and see two more birds fly off. The nest was empty.

When Rasim made his way to the garden, Rosmerta ran to him to tell him the news.

"Praise Allah," he said. "Our babies have grown into strong adults and are ready to face the world. You too, my dear

Rosmerta, are ready to face the world. Are you prepared to become a complete woman?"

This confused her. Surely, after all she had been through, she could no longer be considered an innocent little girl. What more did she have to do to become a woman?

"I know of the trials to which you have been subjected," Rasim said, as if reading her mind. "You have been tested in ways that destroy most people. Allah has great things in store for you. While you are waiting for Allah's plan to be revealed, you must commit yourself to Him."

"What do you mean? What must I do?"

"You must become one of Allah's people. You must express your faith in Him and commit yourself to His work."

Rasim was asking Rosmerta to convert to Islam. Any real faith she had was left behind on the trail of death. Giving up Christianity was not a problem. She could see that this was important to her new family, and she wanted to please them. And yet, somehow, converting to Islam felt like a betrayal of her old family. How could she now say she was a Muslim after all the Muslims had put them through? It occurred to Rosmerta that if her family had converted to Islam before the deportation order, they would all be alive today. Making this statement was Rosmerta's chance for salvation—in a physical sense, anyway. And besides, where was Christ when she had needed him?

"How do I do it? How do I convert?"

Rasim smiled. "It's very easy. I'll file a petition with the court and we will go before the magistrate. He will ask you a few questions, and you will be a proper Muslim woman. You have made me very happy, Rosmerta."

When the day came, Rosmerta and Rasim went to the city hall and stood before a judge, an old man with a short gray beard and piercing dark eyes. She was nervous. She didn't know what to expect. Rasim told her to answer the judge's questions honestly and everything would be okay. Rosmerta's legs felt weak and her knees were bouncing off each other as she faced the judge. He just stared at her. She waited. Finally, he smiled.

"What is your name?"

"Rosmerta Bedrosian."

"You are Armenian?"

"Yes, sir."

"Do you believe in Jesus?"

This was it. It was time. She had to make a commitment. She thought of her father. *"Do what you must do to survive,"* he had said. *"Where there is life, there is hope."* If life required denouncing a god who wouldn't or couldn't help his people, then so be it. Shushawn, if she were still alive, would tell Rosmerta that she could not renounce her Christian faith any more than she could renounce her existence. This was her St. Sarkis moment.

Rosmerta turned to look back at Rasim. He nodded his encouragement. She faced the judge and took a deep breath. She couldn't do it. "Yes," she said, "I believe in Jesus."

"Excellent," said the judge. "So do we."

A wave of relief washed over Rosmerta. Her heart rate slowed to a more reasonable pace and her breathing returned to normal.

"Jesus was a great prophet," the judge continued. "He gave us many important teachings. The second coming of Jesus in Jerusalem will be a critical step in the ultimate destruction of this world, leading to Allah's final judgment. However, Christians have distorted the true teachings of Jesus. In his infinite wisdom, Allah sent his prophet Mohammed, may peace be upon him, to instruct us in the truth. As a Muslim, it is your duty to strive to understand this truth and live your life according to the will of Allah. Do you accept the one true religion? Do you accept Islam?"

"Yes sir," Rosmerta said before she had a chance to think about what she was doing.

"Good," the judge said, still smiling. "Today you are making an important first step on the path of truth. For this new journey, you will need a new name. From now on you will be called Kamelya Sengor."

The judge indicated that the proceedings had come to an end. Rosmerta, now Kamelya, was trembling. Rasim escorted her out of the chambers. Before leaving the building, he pulled a shawl from his coat and presented it to his daughter with pride. "You are now a Muslim woman, Rosmerta. You must dress like one."

Rosmerta was relieved to hear Rasim address her using her Armenian name. She wasn't sure she could get used to being called Kamelya. She placed the scarf over her head and smiled at him. Rasim smiled back. "Now you are ready for anything."

Kaj Returns

Kaj was frustrated. He and his group of accomplices had deserted from the Special Organization more than a month ago. Living on what they could take from the Armenians was a decent life while it lasted—before the caravans had slowed to a trickle. Those refugees who still moved through the countryside didn't carry enough with them to make it worth the effort.

Working freelance had its advantages. The group respected strength and brutality, and as one of the most ruthless killers around, Kaj was a leader. He worked to his own schedule. He got up when he wanted, and his band of hooligans moved on his orders. It was all wonderful, except that recently, his charges were showing signs of restlessness. They were hungry, and supplies were dwindling. Kaj was feeling confident, though. It had taken some persuasion to get the group to follow him this far, but today it would pay off. He had promised a big payday, and now it was time to deliver.

They broke camp early in the morning and started towards the Euphrates River. The bridge across the river provided a nice view of the valley. A gentle flow of water trickled below them. This late in the summer, everything seemed to be a little slower. The water was a clear turquoise with flecks of gold— reflections from the rising sun.

Kaj's band walked over a small hill to see Jerablus below them. The town was quiet, just as he expected. It was time. Kaj gave the order and the gang broke into a jog. When they reached the first house at the outskirts of Jerablus, Kaj called out, "Allahu Akbar!"

"Allahu Akbar," came the reply. Several men crashed through the door to the first house. They moved quickly, taking anything of value and all the food. They were out of the house in minutes, leaving its inhabitants disoriented and frightened. Anyone who showed even the feeblest sign of resistance, or just got in the way, was dispatched with a fierce swing of the sword. At each residence, three or four of Kaj's marauding miscreants peeled off and stormed the poor unsuspecting inhabitants, stole what they could, and rejoined their compatriots. They didn't move towards the center of town for fear of being trapped. It may have been an unnecessary precaution—the action was totally unexpected. When it was over, the gang had collected enough supplies and valuables to satisfy everyone. In Jerablus, they left eighteen Muslims dead and perhaps a hundred injured.

Rosmerta heard the commotion and stayed in her room until it was over. Then she opened the door and went out looking for Rasim. She found him and Zayna holding each other in the garden. "What happened?"

"I'm not sure," said Rasim, letting go of his wife. "There was an attack. Many injured. Umar went to check on Wasim and his family."

"The Russians are here?"

"No," said Rasim. "They were Turks—possibly Turkish soldiers. No one seems to know for sure. It's okay though. They're gone now."

Rosmerta began to shake. She was just beginning to feel safe, and now this.

"It's okay. We're all okay and the thugs are gone."

They went back into the house. Rosmerta joined in a hug with Rasim and Zayna. She was almost calm, when Umar arrived with the news: Wasim and his father were dead, and his mother was missing. Umar thought she was probably kidnapped.

"It's all your fault," Umar told Rosmerta. "The soldiers wouldn't have come if you weren't here. They were looking for Armenians. Wasim was right: we should have left you to die beside the river."

"What a terrible thing to say!" scolded Rasim. "And you know full well that's not true."

"I know no such thing. We were never attacked before she got here. The Turks have been killing Armenians or driving them into the desert for months. We take in one Armenian, and now the Turks are after us."

"That's enough. Rosmerta is part of our family now. Those men weren't after Armenians, they were attacking anyone and everyone. Their aggression had nothing to do with Rosmerta. Now I have to go shopping for tonight's dinner. You leave your sister alone. I'll be back as soon as I can." Rasim headed into town.

Zayna went into the garden, leaving Umar alone with Rosmerta. Umar started to leave too, then thought better of it.

"Why are you here anyway?"

"I don't know. As I understand it, I'm here because you fished me out of the river and brought me here. And I thank you for that."

"You agree that I saved your life? You owe me something, don't you think?" asked Umar as he got closer to Rosmerta.

"Yes, I guess I do," she responded stepping back away from him until she was pressed against the wall. Umar was still coming towards her. "And what is the price you want for saving my miserable Armenian life?"

Umar was now inches in front of Rosmerta. He peered down at the swell of her breasts and leaned in until he could feel them pressing into his chest. "You have filled out nicely. You were very thin when I found you."

Rosmerta glared at him. "What do you want, Umar?"

"I told you," he said, as he slid Rosmerta's dress up her legs.

"No!" she cried when his hands reached her underwear. "Stop."

Umar pulled Rosmerta's underwear down. He grabbed her hard and pushed her against the wall. With his other hand he fumbled to free himself. Rosmerta squirmed and tried to duck under his arm. He was too strong. He put his hand on her throat and squeezed. She tried to pull away, but she succeeded only in smashing her head against the wall. Umar grabbed Rosmerta's shoulders. He extended his right leg and threw her over it. She landed hard on her left side and rolled onto her back. Umar fell on top of her. She thrashed about one last time before he slapped her hard across the face and she gave up. She pleaded while Umar fumbled with his pants again.

"No, please stop! Umar, please. Please stop."

But Umar was intent on finishing what he started. When he was done, he stood up and glared down at Rosmerta. "If you ever tell anyone about this, I will kill you." He walked away, leaving her lying on the floor.

She lay there whimpering for a while, then picked herself up and got back to work. When Zayna returned, Rosmerta fixed dinner and didn't say a word about what happened.

That night, Rosmerta couldn't sleep. She was lying awake, wondering what she should do. She couldn't tell Rasim what happened. Umar was his son, and she was—well, she wasn't his daughter. She couldn't stay here. She had to leave. But where would she go? And how would she survive?

Every thought increased the panic. Then one thought pushed her over the edge: *What if I'm pregnant? No, four boys raped me in Sivas and I didn't get pregnant. Surely one boy here can't manage it. But I was much weaker then. I've recovered and I'm much stronger now. But I can't escape into a world that is doing everything it can to kill me while I'm pregnant. If Adelina couldn't handle it, I certainly can't. I have to stay until I know.*

Rosmerta didn't get much sleep that night, but she knew one thing; she could never be alone with Umar again.

Aleppo

Rasim was smiling. Nonetheless, Rosmerta sensed that something wasn't right. His energy was low, and he was talking more quickly than normal. "We'll be leaving for Aleppo tomorrow," he said.

Rosmerta knew that the Sengor men made frequent trips to Aleppo, but the women never went with them. The Euphrates river ran through Jerablus. The fertile banks of the river were covered with farms growing cotton. Jerablus was a small town with little use for large stocks of cotton. Rasim made a fine living for his family buying up the cotton from local farmers and transporting it to the much larger city of Aleppo where his brother Selim could always find buyers. So travel to Aleppo made perfect sense for the men. But for Rosmerta? "Why do I have to go?"

"Now that you're healthy, you can come with us. It will be good for you to get out of the house."

It still seemed odd. Rosmerta couldn't identify what was making her uncomfortable, but something just didn't feel right.

The next morning, after finishing breakfast, Umar excused himself to get the horses and cart ready for the trip. Zayna departed as well, leaving Rosmerta alone with Rasim. "I have some bad news," he said. "Something has come up, and we can't all go to Aleppo after all."

Rosmerta felt her body relax. She was relieved that she would not be traveling.

Rasim continued, "You and Umar will have to go alone."

Rosmerta tensed again as panic overtook her. Alone with Umar? She had to stop this.

"Umar should have the cart ready by now. Let's get you on your way."

While she was being led to her fate, Rosmerta frantically searched for a way out. "I don't want to go," is all she could muster. She was embarrassed by the fear in her voice.

"It's okay," Rasim reassured her. "Umar has made this trip many times. He knows the way."

"I don't feel well," Rosmerta tried.

"You're just nervous. You'll be fine." Rasim lifted Rosmerta onto the cart beside Umar.

"Peace be upon you, father," Umar said. "I'll be back in a few days." He snapped the reins and they were on their way.

The pair traveled in silence for a while, until Rosmerta couldn't take it any longer. "Tell me about Aleppo. Is it nice?"

"It's one of the oldest cities in the world. People have lived in the area for thousands of years. Alexander the Great took control of Aleppo. Later the Mongols and now the Ottomans. I think at one point Aleppo was even part of the Kingdom of Armenia."

Rosmerta couldn't stop herself from smiling. All the stories her father had told her about the Armenians, and he never mentioned Aleppo. Did he know about it? Probably— he seemed to know about everything.

"Speaking of Armenians," Umar continued. "They built one of those tent settlements for Armenians in Aleppo. You know, where they let your people live. That's probably where they were taking you before you were injured."

"Where they let Armenians live temporarily until they push them out and send them on to the next place, you mean." Rosmerta felt the anger rising inside her. She fought hard to push it back down.

"No," said Umar. "From what I've heard, the camp in Aleppo is the end of the road. It's a permanent settlement where Armenians can live until the war is over and everyone can go home."

The energy in Rosmerta suddenly shifted; anger turned to hope. If this was true—if the Aleppo camp was a settlement where she could stay—then she could get out from under the constant threat she felt living with Umar, and she could live with her own people. She and Umar would be spending several days with his uncle's family before they were scheduled to return to Jerablus. If she could escape and get to the camp, she would be free of this whole mess.

The two continued in silence while Rosmerta considered her options and Umar concentrated on whatever he found interesting.

Rosmerta was pretty sure she knew what Umar found interesting. She also knew they couldn't make the entire journey to Aleppo in one day. They would have to spend the night somewhere. In addition to finding a way to escape to the Armenian settlement, Rosmerta had to come up with a plan to escape Umar tonight.

They made it all the way to al-Bab—well over halfway. They stayed at a small inn, as brother and sister. Umar gazed at Rosmerta with hungry eyes.

"You try anything tonight, and I'll scream. On the way back, I'll do anything you want," Rosmerta told Umar, then she rolled over. It was hard to sleep while listening to the sounds of his deep breathing. Her ploy seemed to work. Umar left her alone for the night.

The next day they approached a huge city, by far the largest Rosmerta had seen. Stone structures came together at odd angles with a tangle of medieval roads twisting their way around the buildings. The skyline was dominated by the Citadel, a walled fortress sitting high on a hill in the middle of the ancient city of Aleppo.

Umar's Uncle Selim lived on the east side of the city with his wife Ferah and their 27-year-old son Bekir in a large stone house. It was a two-story structure. Unlike some homes Rosmerta had seen back in Bayburt, the downstairs area was not dedicated to animals. The entire house was living space for the family.

And what a space it was. Bekir had been educated in Austria. While studying there, he worked for the French embassy. He returned to his family with some strange Western ideas about furnishings. There were chairs and tables and even a bed in Bekir's room. The fact that he had a room to himself didn't seem as strange as it might have before Rosmerta lived with Rasim's family—but a bed? While Bekir's parents gave in to his desire to westernize the common areas of the house, they still slept on the floor. They couldn't understand why anyone would want to sleep on a raised platform covered with a giant pillow.

Bekir's wife Sanya was a pretty enough girl with a long body and short legs. She greeted Umar with a broad smile and a slight bow. "Umar, it is so nice to see you. How is your father? I am so sorry he couldn't make the trip this time. We do so enjoy his visits. Last time, he told us you are still not married. A handsome man like you should have someone by now. You do want a wife, don't you? You will make such a fine husband. Your father is such a nice man, and you obviously take after him."

"Sanya, this is Rosmerta," Umar said, interrupting her.

Sanya's smile disintegrated. She glared at Rosmerta. "Oh," she said. "I know who this is." She turned her back to Rosmerta and walked away.

"Is she always like that?" Rosmerta asked. "Talkative, I mean."

"Yes."

"I don't think she likes me."

"You should be used to that." Umar walked away, leaving Rosmerta standing by herself with an ever-growing crowd gathering before her.

Relatives arrived from all parts of Aleppo. Most of the men went straight to Bekir and slapped him on the back. They seemed to be congratulating him. Rosmerta was too nervous to ask what was happening. Perhaps Sanya was pregnant. That would explain the backslapping and maybe even the reception Sanya had given her.

Dinner was a splendid sequence of peppers stuffed with ground lamb, rice with chicken flavored with pine nuts and roasted almonds, lamb with a minty yogurt sauce, and salads of every description. Pita bread was served with everything. When the meal was complete, Selim called the gathering to order so he could make an announcement. The group hushed in anticipation.

"Friends, thank you for coming. And a special welcome to Umar bin Rasim who has traveled all the way from Jerablus to bring us our newest family member. Welcome to Aleppo, Kamelya."

Everyone nodded at Rosmerta. She scanned the room apprehensively. At first, the name meant nothing to her, then she realized Selim was welcoming her. She hadn't heard her Muslim name since the day she converted. Was she going to have to get used to being called Kamelya now? Rosmerta was glad she wasn't staying long. If she could find the camp, she could disappear back into her own community. It wouldn't take them long to forget her.

"This is a life changing event for my son Bekir," Selim said. "As this will be his second marriage, we can be less formal this time around."

Selim continued to talk and even solicited laughter on occasion. Rosmerta was no longer listening. Very slowly, it began to dawn on her that the reason she was in Aleppo was to marry Bekir. Why hadn't Rasim told her? Why hadn't Umar? Of course, this did explain why Umar had not raped her on the journey from Jerablus. She knew that her ploy was too simple. And it was pretty clear now why Sanya wasn't exactly thrilled to see her. Rosmerta, it seemed, was the fix to whatever problem Sanya had that left Selim without a grandson. Rosmerta was angry and hurt and flabbergasted and... it just wasn't right.

Later, after she calmed down, Rosmerta realized that everyone in Aleppo assumed that she knew why she was here. Apparently, Rasim was supposed to have informed her, but couldn't bring himself to admit to her that he was giving her away. That explained why he had Umar escort her to Aleppo.

Now it was even more important that she find the camp and reestablish herself as Rosmerta Bedrosian, daughter of Megerdich Bedrosian. She was Armenian, Christian, and most definitely not married.

Not Here

Rosmerta was pleased to find that she was to spend the night on the ground floor near the entrance to the house. She waited until everyone was asleep and slipped out. When the sun rose, she crept out from her hiding place behind the neighbor's house and went looking for the camp.

Rosmerta quickly discovered that many of the roads that looked promising at first, abruptly ended after a couple turns. Finding her way around the labyrinth that was the Aleppo road system was going to be difficult.

Through trial and error, she found her way to the edge of town where the camp was set up. It was enormous, the biggest she had seen. A smell of rotting flesh radiated from the camp as she skirted around the edge. A frail woman with only a rag hanging over her shoulders shuffled up to Rosmerta on the opposite side of the fence that encircled the camp, mumbling, "Na he."

"Excuse me?" Rosmerta asked.

"Na he," the old women repeated, holding her left hand up to Rosmerta's face and pointing to her palm with her index finger. "Na he."

"I'm sorry. I don't understand."

"Na he. Na he. Na he."

"Not here?"

The woman nodded vigorously. "Na he."

"Oh," Rosmerta said, "the spots. You have red spots all over your body. Everywhere except the palms of your hands."

The woman nodded and almost smiled. "Na he," she agreed and then shuffled on.

Rosmerta felt sorry for the delirious woman. Nonetheless, she was glad to be rid of her. As she moved along the fence, she saw that many people had the red spots. Some were too weak to get up, some were vomiting. Everyone looked miserable. Rosmerta's mood sank. Umar had said that this was not the usual camp for transient Armenians—it was a semi-permanent settlement. This was the end of the line. And now that she was here, Rosmerta believed it was true. With a Typhus epidemic rampaging through the camp, no further deportation orders were needed. Death was almost certain. Rosmerta had hoped that camp would prove to be a good place to wait for the end of the war and then a relocation to a new life, but the old lady was correct: *"Not here."*

Rosmerta was leaving, when a skinny boy ran up to her, looking excited. His face was sunken into his skull, his eyes bulging out of hollowed sockets. His voice was thin yet somehow familiar.

"Rosmerta, it's me, Boghos!"

She couldn't believe it. Standing in front of her was none other than Boghos Elmassian. Yet, somehow, it wasn't him. Unlike many of his campmates, Boghos seemed to be untouched by Typhus. Still, he was emaciated. There was little of him left. She reached over the fence to hug him. Her arms wrapped around him like he wasn't there. She felt as if she was hugging herself.

"You look amazing, Rosmerta. So healthy, I mean. Where have you been?"

Rosmerta told Boghos about her experiences since the day of their separation at the river. She asked about his time. He said it was more of the same. Rosmerta didn't fully believe him, but decided she knew enough. Boghos confirmed that staying in the camp voluntarily was not a good idea. They decided they would try to get him out.

"Stop!" yelled the guard when Rosmerta and Boghos approached the gate. "Where do you think you're going?"

"I am Kamelya Sengor, daughter of Rasim Sengor from Jerablus. I have come to collect my brother Boghos and take him home."

"You're from Jerablus? I heard there was an attack there?"

"Yes," replied Rosmerta. "Our good friend Abdullah al-Fanari was killed along with his son Wasim."

"It must have been horrifying."

"It has been difficult. Now at least we have our brother returned to us. Now if you would please allow us to pass…"

"Yes, yes of course. My best to your family, young lady."

Rosmerta breathed a sigh of relief as they walked away from the camp. Her shoulders relaxed and she felt the blood rush back into her head. It was only now that she realized how close she had been to passing out.

"Thanks for getting me out," said Boghos. "What are you going to do? Are you going back to your Muslim family, or will you be joining me on the streets of Aleppo?"

"I thought you'd come back to Jerablus with me."

"And how do you plan to explain me to your new family? Am I supposed to convert to Islam?" Boghos shook his head.

"I don't think so. That may be fine for you, but I'm a Christian and I plan to stay a Christian. And taking in a young girl who can become one of many women in a harem is one thing. What are they going to do with me?"

"It's not like that. Rasim is kind to me. He loves me and takes good care of me."

"From what you told me, it was Umar who was taking care of you. Will you be traveling back to Jerablus with him?"

Rosmerta felt the heat of embarrassment rise in her face. She shouldn't have told him. What was she to do? She wasn't going home with Umar, that was certain. The options seemed to be to marry Bekir or to escape. But to where? Staying on the street with Boghos didn't seem like a reasonable option.

"Kamelya, there you are."

Alarmed, Rosmerta nodded at Boghos. "You better go," she whispered as Bekir approached.

"We've been looking for you. Who was that you were with?"

"Oh, no one. Some beggar from the camp."

"They need to do a better job of keeping them contained so they don't spread their diseases all over town."

Rosmerta sulked all the way back to the house. How could she have been so stupid? She had hoped the camp would be her refuge. It wasn't. Still, she could have found another escape. Why had she just stood there and let Bekir take her? Why hadn't she run? And what was all that talk of going back to Jerablus? Rasim had committed Rosmerta to Bekir. If she showed up in Jerablus, he would send her back. So now she would be married to a total stranger in a strange house with a strange family. How could she let this happen? Then again, what else could she do?

Bekir was sulking, too, and considering his soon to be bride. She was going to be a problem. He could see that already. He would have to keep a closer eye on her. It was not acceptable to have your wife wandering around town unescorted, even if it was your second wife. Yes, he must be careful. The first thing he would do was move her to an upstairs bedroom.

Bekir's Wedding

The next day, Rosmerta was cleaned and primped by all the women in the extended family. Even Sanya joined in, taking charge of fixing the bride's hair. After it was cleaned, dried, and brushed, Rosmerta's hair was parted down the middle of her head. Her dark curls framed her face. Sanya pulled a brush through the front half of Rosmerta's hair, causing it to fall in front of her face. She took the scissors and cut above her eyebrows. "There, now you have bangs like a proper Muslim girl." The other women laughed. "You'll like bangs. No more hair falling in your face. You'll be able to see. And Muslim men do prefer women with bangs." Sanya stopped suddenly as if she just remembered who she was talking to.

The celebration would be a small event, attended mostly by the same group from the night Rosmerta arrived. Nothing like the momentous affair that marked the marriage of Sanya and Bekir. Or at least that's what Sanya kept telling her. But as everyone reminded her, this was Bekir's second marriage. So not such a big deal.

Well, it was a big deal to Rosmerta. This Muslim custom of men having multiple wives didn't sit well with her Christian upbringing. But she wasn't Christian anymore, was she? Strange though—she didn't feel any different. She was also marrying someone she didn't know or even know *about* until a couple days ago. Of course, arranged marriages were the norm in Armenian society too, and many Armenian weddings involved people who didn't know each other well. The worst part was that Rosmerta was beginning to understand that she wasn't going to be so much Bekir's wife, as Sanya's slave. This was bad. But again, what could she do? It wasn't as if anyone was asking her opinion on anything.

Rosmerta's conversion to Islam was a farce. She knew that now. She did what she had to do to stay alive—just as Megerdich had taught her. Rosmerta was no more a Muslim than she was a bird. She wasn't sure she was Christian either, but she certainly wasn't Muslim. And she would cooperate with this ceremony because that is what she had to do to survive for today. When it was over, she would—in her own mind, anyway—be no more married than she was a Muslim. She would bide her time and escape when the opportunity arose.

The men left in the morning. Rosmerta was told to stay in her room until Bekir returned. She could hear people gathering in the rooms below her. The general mood seemed to be exuberant and celebratory. Suddenly, a cheer went up and someone yelled, "Bekir!"

The entire house pulsed with the rhythmic stomping. Rosmerta could hear the ruckus getting louder as it moved towards her.

The door opened and Bekir walked in. Another cheer went up as he closed the door, separating himself and Rosmerta from the noisy crowd.

"We're married now," Bekir said simply.

"Married? How? Nothing has happened yet."

"In our culture, men fill out the paperwork and file it with the authorities and the marriage is official. That's all done. It's all over. Well, except for one part."

After witnessing the elaborate ceremonies associated with Armenian weddings in Bayburt, this all seemed very small and insignificant. Apparently, they were married now, and now, Bekir wanted to act as a husband acts to his new bride.

It was quick and easy, nothing too horrible. When he was done, Bekir checked to see if there was blood. He didn't seem very surprised when he found none. He simply grunted and straightened his clothes. He walked over to a small box near the doorway, pulled out a knife and a small square of white cloth. Bekir approached the bed holding the knife in front of him.

Rosmerta searched for an escape. A wall blocked her path to the left. Bekir was coming from the right. She tried to slither down the bed, but Bekir grabbed her arm and pushed her back up. She kicked and flailed about, pushing her back against the headboard. There was nowhere to go. She was trapped in her own bedroom. Her head swung back and forth as she searched for a weapon.

Bekir laughed. "Relax. It's not as if I'm going to kill you."

Rosmerta stopped moving even though his words did not comfort her. She sat in the bed, shaking in fear, waiting for her fate to unfold.

Bekir rested the knife against Rosmerta's ankle, flicked it, and held the cloth over it until a small red stain appeared. He returned the knife to the box.

Bekir left the room holding up the bloody cloth. There was another great cheer and then the noise moved away from the bedroom, towards the party downstairs.

Rosmerta was left to herself. She could hear singing and dancing. It didn't seem that anyone cared whether she joined her own wedding celebration or not. After sitting alone for a long time, she couldn't take it anymore. She pulled herself off the bed and walked down to celebrate with her new family.

When she reached the bottom of the stairs, Rosmerta was surprised to find that there was not so much one celebration as two. The main room on the ground floor was divided by a curtain. On one side, she could see the women dancing and singing. On the other side were the men. Both groups seemed to be enjoying themselves, but there was no interaction between them. It was as if they were two separate, unrelated groups that just happened to be in the same building, celebrating their separate, unrelated accomplishments at the same time.

While there were some obvious differences between what Rosmerta was accustomed to and the Syrian wedding— singing and the separation of the sexes primary among them— there were also many similarities. Dancing was an important part of any Armenian celebration. At an Armenian wedding, everyone formed a big circle and performed prescribed movements in an agreed upon order. This Syrian dancing seemed to be pure chaos. If there was any pattern in it, Rosmerta couldn't decipher it. Luckily, no one seemed inclined to invite her to participate.

The most obvious similarity between an Armenian and Syrian party was the abundance of food. Rosmerta saw savory pies, steamed turkey, fried partridge, artichokes, and a variety of fresh fruits for dessert. In many ways, it was exactly what she had dreamed about for months while she was wandering around Anatolia. Now that she had it, Rosmerta found no comfort in it. Being able to eat her fill was wonderful of course, and she would never take that for granted again. Nonetheless, the whole affair was so strange and foreign that it left her feeling disoriented and ill.

Married Life

Rosmerta adjusted to her new life. As she expected, Sanya stopped doing much of anything except bossing her around. She was almost beginning to think that Sanya enjoyed having her there. But every few nights, Bekir would take Rosmerta to his room. Sanya put on a brave face, but Rosmerta knew it killed her to see her husband going upstairs to be with another woman. The next day, Sanya was always just a little more demanding than usual.

It wasn't as if Rosmerta enjoyed the nights with Bekir. She couldn't call it rape—they were married, after all—but it wasn't exactly an act of love, either. What bothered her more than anything else was that all Bekir wanted out of this arrangement was a son, and the last thing Rosmerta wanted right now was to get pregnant.

After a few months, Rosmerta started to believe she might not be able to get pregnant. Perhaps all the abuse her body had taken along the caravan route was just too much, and now she couldn't have a baby. Once this possibility started to work its way into her mind, she almost wanted to get pregnant. Not that she wanted a baby, and she certainly didn't want to carry Bekir's child, she just wanted to know that she *could*.

Then she was pregnant, and she wished she wasn't. There were, however, certain advantages. Once Bekir learned that Rosmerta was with child, she became the preferred wife. Suddenly he was instructing Sanya to do all the work. Rosmerta was to rest and take care of his son.

On the other hand, Rosmerta's every move was being watched. In Bayburt, she had traveled around town with Megerdich. They visited shops that were generally reserved for men, but he took her with him anyway. They went from home to home to discuss the town's affairs. Rosmerta loved to see the respect and admiration everyone showed her father.

In Jerablus, Rosmerta almost never left the house, but she had spent many hours sitting in the courtyard with Rasim. She cherished her time with her second father. Like Megerdich, Rasim knew about the world and was happy to teach Rosmerta what he knew.

But here in Aleppo, she was an outcast. Even pregnant with Bekir's child, she was still treated like some sort of foreign invader. Almost all her interactions were with the other women of the family, who kept an eye on Rosmerta and were more than happy to tell her whenever she did something wrong. The men—even Bekir—had little to do with any of the women, especially Rosmerta.

Rosmerta was lonely. She missed the men who had guided her in the past. She missed seeing the world outside the four walls of Selim's house. It was strange that, after all the hardship she experienced out in the world, now that she was safely tucked inside, all she wanted was to get back out. And now that she was pregnant, she had fewer chances than ever to do that. She was grateful to be alive when so many had lost that opportunity. Still, she hated living like this, trapped with women who wanted her here even less then she wanted to be here.

But even the most careful observation couldn't keep Rosmerta under surveillance all the time. Eventually, she found a weakness in the perimeter. One day, Sanya went upstairs thinking Ferah was still watching Rosmerta, but Ferah was on her way back to the storage area to get rice for the evening meal. Rosmerta acted quickly. She was out the door almost before Sanya was out of her sight. She wasn't sure where she was going. She didn't have a plan. She only knew she had to get away and explore. Not that she did not intend to escape—she did—just not now. Life on the streets alone was hard enough. Add pregnancy, and it was a recipe for disaster. Somewhere in the back of her mind, Rosmerta knew that someday she would escape for real, and the more she knew about Aleppo before then, the better. For now, she wandered the streets and tried to find a few landmarks. The Citadel, sitting atop its mound, was the first obvious one. If she moved towards it, towards the center of town, she was moving away from the camp. She had to avoid the camp at all cost.

Near the house, many small streets intersected at strange angles in a confusing mess that Rosmerta was sure she would never decipher. But a short distance away, she found some wide thoroughfares, lined on both sides by busy shops. Patrons flowed in and out of stores that sold everything Rosmerta could imagine and some things she could never have believed existed. Above the shops were housing units where Rosmerta guessed the shop keepers probably lived.

With the constant flow of horse drawn carriages and pedestrians, Rosmerta was confident she could remain inconspicuous here.

"Rosmerta?"

She jumped and let out a sharp squeal. Her body tingled with panic. She turned to see a young man rushing towards her with a big smile. He gave her a warm hug and stepped back. It was Boghos. He looked much better now. His face was fuller, and he even had a thin beard sprouting on his chin. He was wearing clean clothing with sandals. He even had a fez on his head.

Rosmerta couldn't keep herself from laughing. "What's with the hat? You look like a proper Muslim man."

"Just trying to fit in," he said defensively.

"You look much better. Where are you staying?"

"Nowhere."

"You're living on the streets?"

"Yeah, I love it. No one tells me what to do. I do what I want."

"If you're living by yourself on the street, where did you get that outfit?"

"What does it matter? I get what I need, when I need it. You should join me."

"I can't. If I try to escape, Bekir will kill me."

"Then why are you out here? Why did you leave at all if you're just going back?"

It was a question she was asking herself, too. She needed time to think. "I have to get back. I think I can get out again." She hoped this was true. "Where can we meet?"

"Follow me. I'll show you my favorite place in town."

Rosmerta walked with Boghos to the next intersection and turned the corner. A couple blocks down the street, a stone tower ascended proudly from the center of a wide, open square at the intersection of several streets. With a slight flare at the base, the square tower rose skyward. About halfway up, an elaborately decorated walkway progressed around the structure. Above the walkway, each face of the tower presented a large clock face. Above that, the honeycomb vaulting of a *muqarnas* narrowed to a small dome capped by a metal sculpture that reminded Rosmerta of a cross. Maybe that's what it was, but it seemed out of place. Or maybe it was Rosmerta who seemed out of place.

As they got closer it became obvious that the topper was a wind indicator, pointing into the light breeze that cooled the square.

"We can meet at the clock tower," said Boghos. "When do you think you can get out again?"

"In a few days—three days. At midday. That will be after breakfast is done and before I have to start working on dinner. Can you be there then?"

"Of course. I told you, I can do anything I want."

"Okay. I'll see you in three days."

Rosmerta was concerned about making this commitment. She didn't want to tell Boghos that she wasn't sure if she could get out to see him again. He would think she was being held against her will, and that would not be entirely untrue.

As it turned out, escaping wasn't hard after all. When Rosmerta got back to the house, the women acted as if they didn't know she had been gone. She knew this was unlikely. Three days later, she tried it again. This time Rosmerta was sure the women had intentionally given her the opportunity.

Did they want her to leave? Maybe they hoped Bekir would catch her outside the house. Then she would be in serious trouble. Or maybe they hoped something would happen to her while she was wandering around on her own. Maybe they thought she would escape and then she would be out of their lives forever. Whatever the reason, Rosmerta soon found that the gauntlet she had been subjected to had broken down, and whenever the men were gone, the women seemed to find things to do in other parts of the house, leaving Rosmerta free to slip out and see Boghos.

When she did, Boghos was usually wearing new clothing. He always appeared well and impeccably clean. One time, he was wearing a short smock-like Buster Brown suit with long stockings that came over his knees, up to his bloomer pants. "What kind of an outfit is that?" she mused.

"American, I think," he answered cagily.

"American? Where are you getting American clothes?"

Boghos didn't respond.

Something wasn't right. "No, seriously, where are you getting all of these clothes?" Rosmerta pressed.

Boghos shrugged. "You have your Muslim family, I have my own sources. And there's plenty for you, too. You should join me. We can take on the world together."

Rosmerta considered things for a moment. She still hadn't told Boghos she was pregnant. She wasn't showing yet, but she would be soon, and she wanted to tell him before he figured it out on his own. She wanted to leave with him, but there was no way she was going to leave her baby behind. She wanted this baby! She needed to tell Boghos. "We would need to leave Aleppo. I don't like it here. Where could we go?"

"Where would you like to go? We can go anywhere. Tell me where and I'll set it up."

No, this just isn't right. She decided to wait and tell him later. "You talk a lot, Boghos, but let's face it, if you could go anywhere you wanted, you wouldn't still be here."

"I'm doing fine here. I'm surviving on my own terms. If later I decide I want to go somewhere else, then I'll go. For now, I'm fine where I am."

"Yeah, okay, I'll see you around."

"Yeah, you too. And don't forget—anywhere you want. Let me know and I'll set it up."

Rosmerta left Boghos behind and turned down the first side street she came to. She waited, then tentatively she peeked around the corner. Boghos was still standing there where she left him. After a few more minutes, he walked away. She followed him, being careful to avoid detection. Boghos wandered around town for hours. He didn't do anything. He didn't talk to anyone. He just walked and walked.

Finally, as the sun was setting, he made his way to the back of an American-run orphanage. There was a tall stone wall around the grounds. Boghos stopped, looked both ways, then used his arms to pull himself up a small tree while walking up the wall. He scaled the wall and into the compound. He was gone for about ten minutes, then Rosmerta saw Boghos come back over the wall, slide down the tree, and run into the night. He was carrying a loaf of bread and a wool blanket. She didn't dare run after him.

When they met again two days later, he was wearing a wool sports jacket with broad black and orange vertical stripes. There were three buttons in the front with a single pocket high on the left chest and two lower down on either side where Boghos planted his hands.

"I know where you're getting your clothes," said Rosmerta. "And the food too."

"Oh?" said Boghos. "Then you know that there's an infinite supply."

"You're stealing from orphans," she scolded.

"Not stealing," he protested. "The food and clothing are for orphans. I *am* an orphan. I'm taking what was meant for me in the first place."

"Then why don't you stay at the orphanage like the others?" Rosmerta stopped herself from saying "the other children" just in time.

"No way. The orphanage might as well be another camp. I've had enough of those places. Besides, it's less expensive for the orphanage this way. I don't take up any space. They don't have to care for me or worry about what I'm up to. I get what I need and take care of myself."

"That doesn't change the fact that you're stealing."

"I told you, I'm not stealing."

"Then why do you have to sneak in and out? If you're not stealing, why don't you just walk through the front gate like everyone else?"

"How do you know I don't?"

"Because I've seen you. You go to the back and climb up the wall using that tree."

"You followed me? Are you going to turn me in now?" Boghos scowled. "That's okay, I'm leaving anyway. I've had enough of Aleppo. It's time to move on."

"And go where?"

"What difference does it make to you?"

"I want to go with you. I need to get out of here too."

"Are they mistreating you?"

"No, nothing like that. It's just that, it's not my life. It's what they want. I want to live the way I want to live. They tell me what to do all the time. It's as bad as being on the marches, you know?"

"Yes, I do know."

Rosmerta knew he did. "You'll let me come with you?"

"Yes, but I'll need your help. I can get clothing for both of us, but the only food I can get is bread. They leave some on the shelf outside the kitchen in the orphanage. Everything else is locked up. Can you bring food?"

"Yes, I do a lot of the cooking. But I can't leave now." She rested her hand on her swelling abdomen. "How much food do we need anyway?"

"Enough to last both of us for four days."

"There will be three of us," she said, patting her belly.

"Why?"

"Boghos, I'm pregnant."

He just stared at her in stunned silence.

"We have to wait until the baby is born. Then the three of us can leave together."

"We can't take a baby"

"I'm not leaving him behind."

"How are we going to take care of a baby?"

"*We* won't. *I* will. The baby is coming with us." Rosmerta turned and left abruptly.

Motivation

The next few months passed slowly. As Rosmerta's middle expanded, her opportunities to slip away contracted. She didn't really want to leave right now anyway. While she was pregnant, the women took care of her and didn't expect her to perform the difficult chores. She still helped with meal preparation and did some light cleaning and that was about it. Mostly, she was required to rest and take good care of Bekir's child—a boy, he always told her, though she was hoping for a girl. She wasn't sure why. Girls' lives were so restricted by customs. Boys had much more freedom. Maybe it was just because Bekir wanted a boy. In fact, no one seemed to want her to have a girl.

"A girl? Why would you want a girl?" taunted Sanya. "Boys will marry and bring women into the house to help us. Girls require constant training. And just when they become useful, they get married and run off to work for some other family."

Rosmerta tried to ignore her and get on with mixing herbs into a thick yogurt.

Sanya wouldn't let it go. "Girls are useless. They suck up all your time. Once boys grow up, they go out and help the men to bring home money. Girls need constant attention. They can never leave the house. You have to watch them all the time. Turn your back for a moment, and they make a mess. Say anything about it, and they start crying. They cry and they cry. They won't stop. They scream and carry on for hours. You can't stop them. They're horrible."

Bekir stormed into the kitchen. "What are you carrying on about? Don't you ever shut up? I've had it with you!"

"You're drunk again. Where have you been? You know alcohol is forbidden."

"Oh, shut up, you old goat! You can't forbid me." Bekir reached for Sanya's throat.

She ducked under his arm and stuck out her tongue.

Bekir swung his arm out wide, back-handing Sanya in the face.

Sanya staggered away from Bekir, blood flowing from her nose and mouth. She ran up the stairs, holding her hands to her face.

Bekir turned to Rosmerta. He stumbled, then moved towards her. He looked down at her belly and stopped. "What are you looking at?" he yelled, then stormed back out.

Rosmerta stood in shocked silence. She had never seen anyone drunk before. In spite of all the horrors she had endured, she didn't think she had seen anyone quite this angry either—especially not someone she lived with. She knew that if she hadn't been pregnant, she would have been Bekir's next target. She returned to her yogurt. She was trembling with fear. Sanya didn't seem surprised to see Bekir like this. Maybe this was normal for him. The more she thought about it, the more scared she became.

Muslims aren't supposed to drink, but Bekir drank anyway. "You're drunk again," Sanya had said, as if this was not unusual for him.

I have to get out of here, Rosmerta thought. *I have to get out of here now!* It was time to find Boghos and leave. Food...she was supposed to be getting food ready.

From then on, while Rosmerta was helping Ferah prepare dinner, she considered every ingredient. Would this be a good thing to take? Would it spoil before she left? Rosmerta knew she should take beans and vegetables. She was worried about taking meat because someone would notice that. Nutritionally, though, isn't that what they needed for a long walk?

Then there was the actual deed of stealing. How could she take anything without being caught? Wouldn't Ferah notice that it was gone? How could she hide it? She would have to slip it into her clothing while Ferah wasn't looking, then find a place to store everything until the time came. But where? Rosmerta didn't know where to squirrel away her spoils. Therefore, there was no point in taking anything tonight.

As she tried to fall asleep that night, Rosmerta was furious with herself. For dinner, they had lamb with lentils and yogurt. It was almost the perfect meal, yet she had saved none of it. What was she waiting for?

Something better, thought Rosmerta. *Better than lentils? There is nothing better than lentils. They are packed with nutrients. They store easily and are almost indestructible. What could be better?*

The next night, Rosmerta helped Ferah prepare lettuce with fresh cut parsley in a sweet dressing with cracked wheat, diced tomatoes, onions, and olive oil. She had decided she would take a small amount of one thing every night. Tonight, it would be cracked wheat. That would be a sensible start. She separated a large pile of wheat into three piles as she'd been taught, making one a little bigger than the other two. When Ferah turned her back, Rosmerta took a cotton rag from under her shift and held it below the edge of the table in her left hand while using her right hand to sweep the excess portion from the third pile into it. She tied a knot in the rag and slipped it back into her shift. Rosmerta's heart was pounding. Her hands were shaking, and she was sweating all over.

"Are you okay, honey?" Ferah asked when she turned around. "You look terrible."

Rosmerta jumped and nearly knocked a jug of olive oil off the table. "Yes, yes I'm fine." She directed her attention to her work, tossing the tomatoes and onions frantically, all the while feeling Ferah's eyes on her. After what seemed like a very long time, Ferah got back to her own duties and Rosmerta tried to act normal. It was the longest night she could remember since the march.

The next day, when panic began to overwhelm her again, Rosmerta remembered eating bugs and grass and walking through fields of dead bodies. If she had to steal a little food to avoid that, then so be it.

She never got comfortable stealing, but every day it got a little easier. After a week, she had everything they would need except the meat. While preparing lamb kebabs, Rosmerta slipped a few pieces of lamb into an awaiting rag satchel.

"I saw that!" said Sanya, entering the house after fetching water from the well. "Now you're in real trouble. You have no idea. Salim will be furious. He won't tolerate stealing, especially not from you."

Sanya grabbed Rosmerta by the arm and dragged her to Selim. She explained the situation to him while Rosmerta squirmed and awaited her fate. She wasn't sure what was in store for her. But how bad could it really be? After all she had been through, what could they do to her that would compare to what she had already survived?

After hearing the story, Selim thought about it for a while. He scrutinized Rosmerta. "Is this true? Did you steal lamb from the family?"

Rosmerta nodded.

"Do you understand that meat is very difficult to come by right now? That we need everything we can get just to survive? Do you understand why Sanya is angry?"

Again, Rosmerta nodded.

"I know that you suffered greatly during the deportations. I know that you were deprived of the most basic of necessities. We understand," he said, glancing at Sanya, "that because of the hardships you have endured you might feel the need to horde food and supplies. But it is not necessary. If we share what we have, there will be plenty for all of us. You are part of our family now, Kamelya. We won't allow you to starve."

Sanya snorted in disgust.

"You are Bekir's wife, therefore it will be up to him to decide your punishment," said Selim.

"I'm sure he will be fair. Now return to the kitchen and finish preparing dinner."

Sanya smiled, her eyes sparkling with malice. All was not lost after all. Bekir would see reason and provide the discipline that his errant young wife needed.

That night, over dinner, Bekir learned about her treachery. He stayed calm and informed the others that he would deal with it. Sanya was fuming.

After eating, Bekir followed Rosmerta up to her room. He grabbed her arm and spun her around so she was looking at him. He slapped her hard across the face and pushed her against the wall. She fell to the floor. He grabbed a handful of hair and pulled until Rosmerta was on her feet. Then Bekir threw Rosmerta across the room. She slammed into the wall face first and fell down backwards. She scurried back to her feet before Bekir could lift her by her hair again. He punched her in the face and threw her down. He grabbed her hair and pulled her up again. Bekir leaned in close until his nose was almost touching hers and screamed, "Don't you ever embarrass me like that again! If I ever catch you stealing from me again, I will kill you. Do you understand?"

Rosmerta said nothing. Bekir slapped her again. "Do you?"

"Yes," Rosmerta wailed.

"Good," snarled Bekir. Then he punched her once more for good measure.

Rosmerta watched Bekir leave. Then she collapsed into a heap on the floor.

A sharp pain in her abdomen woke Rosmerta. She gasped for air and rolled in agony, her knees pulled up to her chest. Ferah heard her scream and ran to help her. She tried to hold

Rosmerta steady as she thrashed from side to side. Several drops of blood appeared between Rosmerta's legs. Her pleading eyes looked at the blood then up into Ferah's face and back to the blood. Fear gripped her as the spots of blood grew into puddles. A sudden shock of pain ripped through Rosmerta, followed by a fist-sized clot, and then relief.

"You lost the baby," Ferah said.

The ache in her neck and jaw stopped Rosmerta from responding. Her left eye was swollen and black. She tried to get up. That hurt, too. Bekir's beating was worse than she had thought.

Then she remembered Boghos. She needed to see him. How long would he wait for her before leaving Aleppo? Was he worried? Would he come looking for her? Did he even know where she lived? She hoped not. There was no telling what would happen to Boghos if he showed up at the house. Rosmerta tried to think of something else. Her hand moved instinctively to her face, bringing back the pain.

"Why?" It was the question that came to her mind most often these days. Why was she in Aleppo? Why was she married to a Muslim man? Why was she even alive? So many had died, yet here she was. Why her? Why not Shushawn? Shushawn was a better Christian then she ever was. Shushawn was dead. Why not her father? Megerdich was a better person than anyone she knew. He was dead. And what about baby Megerdich? What evil could a baby have committed? The baby was dead. And now her baby, too. She didn't even have time to name him. Or maybe it was a girl. It didn't matter. Her baby was dead like everyone else she knew.

Except for Boghos, she reminded herself. What if he had already left? Rosmerta began to cry. It was all so overwhelming, and so unfair.

Escape

After a couple days, Rosmerta's bruises were a yellow-green and black collage all over her body. Most of the pain had subsided and, except for the swelling around her left eye, her face was back to its normal size if not its normal coloring. She had to find Boghos. She knew that if she left the house, she could never return.

She slid a scarf over her head and pulled it down over her face. She retrieved her hoard from its hiding place and slipped out.

She found Boghos standing at the base of the Bab al-Faraj Clock Tower, as they had agreed. Had he been hanging out here every day for all these months?

"Where have you been?" Despite her attempts to conceal her battered face, Boghos noticed her condition. He froze in shock and anger. "What happened to you?"

"It's nothing," said Rosmerta, looking down at her feet. "Look, I have food," she said, reaching for her satchel.

"Nothing? Your eye is almost swollen shut! Can you even see out of it?"

"I can see fine. It's not as bad as it looks."

"Wait! What about the baby? Did you have it?"

"I don't want to talk about it."

"You should be showing by now... or have given birth. Where's the baby?"

"There is no baby. Okay? No baby," Rosmerta shouted. "It's just the two of us. That's the way you wanted it, right? And we have to leave now. I'm not going back to that house."

"Of course not," he agreed. "But we can't leave yet. We're not ready."

"You may not be ready, but I am. Are you coming with me or not?"

"We're going together, but not today. We'll stay on the street for a day or two and get ready, and then we'll leave."

"If I stay in Aleppo, Bekir will find me and he'll kill me. I'm going." Rosmerta turned and started walking away from Boghos.

"Okay, okay! We'll leave tomorrow. One day. We can wait just one day."

Rosmerta kept walking.

"Rose, this is crazy. We're not ready."

Rosmerta kept walking. Boghos followed. "Okay, we'll leave today. But we need to go north. We'll get outside of town and jump on a train to the coast where we can find a boat to take us out of this dump." He pulled on her arm. "Come on, this way."

They walked through town, dodging masses of people. Rosmerta felt conspicuous at first. Surely everyone could tell she was up to something. She began to see that on the streets of Aleppo, people with many different looks felt perfectly at home. There were elegantly dressed women adorned with gold necklaces, earrings, and stacks of heavy gold bracelets. There were women wrapped in long black gowns that covered everything except their eyes. Women in brightly colored European dresses walked beside tattooed Bedouin women.

As cosmopolitan as the city felt, Rosmerta was still concerned that she was being watched. Every time she saw a man's face, she was sure it was Bekir. It never was. But soon she and Boghos reached the edge of town and started into the desert. No one followed.

Rosmerta was finally comfortable. They had done it. They escaped. It was over. The relief was like coming up for air after being held under water too long. Then she registered the expression on Boghos' face. "What?" she asked. "What's wrong?"

"Nothing. We just need to find the tracks."

They went east for a short distance until they came upon the railroad tracks, then headed north, following the tracks away from town.

The air was still and the sun hot. Walking through the desert brought back many memories. Bad memories. The pair traveled in silence. The sun was past its zenith and moving back towards the horizon, but the peak heat of the day was still hours away. In spite of it all, Rosmerta was excited—they were on their way. Boghos still appeared nervous.

"Don't worry," Rosmerta assured him, "the train will come."

"What about water? Do you have any?"

"No, do you?"

Boghos did not respond. Rosmerta began to consider other things they didn't have, like blankets or extra clothing. The desert would get cold at night. And those lentils she was carrying—how would they cook them? They had no pots, no water, and no fire. Boghos was right. They weren't ready for this trip. They needed that train.

After walking several hours, Boghos felt a vibration that made him jump. He turned to see a train approaching from behind. "There!" he said. "It's coming."

Rosmerta looked back. In the distance she saw a small black dot with a puff of smoke rising from it. The train was a long way away. They stopped and waited.

The vibration became stronger, then they could hear the engine. The dot was growing larger with each puff of smoke.

The noise was almost deafening when the train finally reached them. The small platforms at the ends of each car were high off the ground. The train was both faster and bigger than Rosmerta had anticipated. This was not going to be easy.

Boghos started jogging beside the train. Rosmerta ran behind him. He jumped. His torso landed on the platform, his legs dangling from it. He pulled himself up onto the train.

Rosmerta was too far behind Boghos to jump on the same car. She stopped and waited to jump onto the next one. Like Boghos, only her upper body ended up on the platform. Her arms flailed away as she tried to grab ahold of anything, while her legs kicked wildly, as if to find something to push off. It didn't work. Her body swung around, pulling her off the platform. She fell hard beside the tracks.

Rosmerta sat up, her head pounding. She saw Boghos jump down from the train and run towards her. She tried to get up. Her right ankle collapsed under her weight and she fell again.

"Are you okay?" Boghos screamed over the sounds of the train.

"I'm so sorry." Rosmerta was crying

"Don't worry about that. Are you hurt?"

"My leg hurts."

"Can you walk on it?"

"I don't know."

Boghos put his arm around Rosmerta and helped her up. She screamed when her right leg took her weight. With help, she managed to stay on her feet. She leaned heavily on Boghos and took a few steps. Tears were running down her face.

"I'm so sorry. I couldn't do it. You should have stayed on the train. At least you could have gotten away."

"Don't worry, Rose. We'll find another way."

They continued to struggle along, following the tracks, hoping to find a place to rest. The desert kept going—barren wasteland as far as the eye could see. Boghos changed direction. Rosmerta followed. They walked for a while before she saw what had attracted his attention. Two scrubby little bushes sat alone at the edge of a small rock ledge. As they got closer, Rosmerta could see that there were patches of grass in the area as well. They ripped up handfuls of grass and chewed them enthusiastically. It wasn't much, but the moisture they could squeeze from the grass was at least a temporary relief.

Boghos knelt beside one of the bushes and started digging for water. He turned up only dry earth. They collected as much grass as they could and started moving again.

It was a long afternoon. The sun was hot, though not as hot as Rosmerta remembered it being the last time she walked through the desert. The grass helped. The day ended with a magnificent display of color. The sunset was a progression from a soft yellow to a bright orange and finally a hot red. Rosmerta was almost mesmerized by nature's beauty.

They found a small rock formation that stood up above the dry earth and rested against it. They tried to eat Rosmerta's hard biscuits. Without water, they only managed a few bites. They laid back and tried to get some sleep.

Other than the cold of the night, Rosmerta and Boghos found their desert campsite to be comfortable. The night noises were familiar in a distant, dreamy way. Many creatures spend the hot day buried in the earth and come out at night in search of food—not a problem, as long as they kept their distance. Rosmerta was about to fall asleep when one of them ran over her leg. All hope for rest disappeared.

They were still exhausted when light appeared on the horizon. They decided to get moving while it was cool. They worked their way back to the tracks and continued to follow them north. Rosmerta's ankle hurt, but she forced herself to keep moving.

They walked past two bodies deteriorating in the hot sun. They tried hard to ignore them. A couple miles further on, they saw another body. Boghos stopped.

"Come on, Boghos. Leave the dead alone," Rosmerta said.

"No. Look." Boghos was pointing to a pile of excrement a few feet from the body.

"Oh great," said Rosmerta.

"No. Look." He walked over to the pile of dried feces and knelt down. He plucked something out of it then picked up the whole pile and broke it into pieces. He picked up a few more things from the debris.

"Oh, come on, Boghos. Let's go."

"Money," he said. "Four gold coins. Here, you take two and I'll keep two. When we get back to civilization, these will come in very handy."

"Yes, they will," Rosmerta agreed. She wasn't thrilled about the source, but she knew full well how much money would help them in town. They continued along the path.

"This way you have some and I have some. If something happens to one of us, or if one of us loses the money for some reason, then the other one still has some."

"Yeah, I get it. Now let's get going. I don't like it here."

By noon, the pain in Rosmerta's ankle and the ferocious heat was too much. She stopped and sat on the ground.

Boghos sat next to her. He didn't let on, but he was relieved to have a break. They had been walking for hours and he needed a rest. They both fell asleep.

A faint light in the western sky was all that remained of the day when Rosmerta came to. Boghos was already awake and seemed to be staring into the distance.

"Do you see it?" he asked.

"See what?"

"There. In the sunset. It looks like a town."

Sure enough, Rosmerta was able to make out a small cluster of artificial lights shining in the distance. Or was she just seeing what Boghos told her to see? Was anything actually there?

They each ate another piece of dry bread and a few nuts before resuming their journey. The tracks were leading them towards the lights. Rosmerta stumbled almost on the first step. The pain in her feet was excruciating. She kicked off her shoes. The relief was immediate. It occurred to her that, once again, she was walking barefoot through the desert. And this time no one had forced her to do it. She had done this to herself.

Soon the lights pierced through the darkness, and they were sure they were moving towards a town. It was still miles away. If they could get there, they could find help.

It was the middle of the night when they arrived. They found a well and drank their fill of water. They dunked the last pieces of bread into the water and utterly consumed them.

They were starting to feel almost normal when a voice called out in the darkness. "What are you doing here?"

"Just getting water," said Boghos. "Then we'll be on our way."

"Enough!" screamed the voice. "Get back where you belong."

"Yes sir." Boghos grabbed Rosmerta's arm and they hurried away from the well.

"Not that way," said the voice. The man approached them, pointing. "That way."

"Yes sir," said Boghos as they turned and started in the direction of the outstretched finger.

"And don't let me catch you out here again!"

As they stumbled into the darkness, Rosmerta felt an icy cold dread. Something wasn't right. She looked back. The man was following them.

"No," came the voice again. "That way," said the man, pointing to his left. Ahead of them was a cluster of tents. Once again, they would be in one of the filthy camps. Too tired to run and too weak to fight, Rosmerta and Boghos entered the camp and searched for a place to spend the night.

A'zaz

Like the town of A'zaz in which it sat, the camp was small—only a few hundred people. Nothing like the one in Aleppo with tens of thousands of residents. People here were not healthy by any normal standards. Nonetheless, they didn't seem to be as thoroughly destroyed as the Bayburt refugees had been when they got this far south. Perhaps they hadn't traveled as far. Or maybe their minders weren't as ruthless. Whatever the reason, this group was relatively well off. They even shared their food.

While Rosmerta was grateful for the generosity, she didn't want to take time to get to know anyone. This was a nice enough camp, but a camp nonetheless. What was the point to making friends with people who wouldn't be alive in a couple weeks? Besides, she and Boghos weren't staying anyway. A couple days to recover and they would escape again and… and what? Whatever it was—wherever it ended—she knew they weren't staying here to die.

Rosmerta was partially correct. She was given one day to recover. The second morning, a group of camel riding gendarmes rounded up the camp and they were back on the trail. The sharp ankle pain from a couple days ago was replaced by a dull ache that Rosmerta found tolerable. Her greatest concern was where they were going. She knew she couldn't keep this up for long, and she certainly couldn't manage another trip into the mountains. Soon after leaving A'zaz, it all became clear. They were going back to Aleppo.

The trip took just one day. One exceedingly long day. Eight hours of stifling hot air sucking the breath out of her lungs. Eight hours of shuffling on super-heated dirt on bare feet and a sore ankle. In spite of it all, Rosmerta was in better shape than some of the other travelers, allowing her to stay in the middle of the pack and avoid any unwelcome attention from the gendarmes.

Boghos, on the other hand, was his usual belligerent self. He wandered away. Rosmerta didn't know where he was or what he was doing. When he rejoined her shortly before they arrived in Aleppo, he seemed contrite. Rosmerta knew that something had happened, but she didn't think it was wise to ask about it. They entered the giant, lice-infested, typhus-ridden Aleppo camp in complete silence.

They were directed to a section where all the tents were green. Rosmerta had never fully understood the color-coding system. She knew that the black tents were where those with typhus and other incurable diseases stayed. As bad as this place was, everyone had a tent to sleep in and food was available. And the condition of the camp was mostly due to the condition of the people in it. The condition of the people was due to the treatment they received before they arrived.

Aleppo was unfortunate to be on the receiving end of the Turks' orchestrated nightmare. Not that the Syrians were particularly nice to the Armenians, or that they didn't commit their own offenses, but they weren't responsible for the whole mess, either. Even the Turks were not all complicit. Without the help of Muhammad Kasaba, the Elmassians wouldn't have gotten the head start they did, and Boghos would have been beheaded by Ahmet. And without Dr. Tarik, Megerdich wouldn't have survived 1895, and then Rosmerta wouldn't be here. And without Rasim Sengor, or even Umar for that matter, Rosmerta could have died.

Of course, she had also run into the Special Organization that attacked defenseless civilians without provocation and the Muslim men who believed they had a right to claim any non-Muslim woman they wanted and force themselves on her for a night or for a lifetime as they saw fit. What made some people risk their own lives to save a complete stranger while others would kill that same stranger just for fun? Why would one person hide a defenseless civilian while others would look for any chance to take advantage of her? None of it made sense. None of it mattered right now either. What mattered now was that Rosmerta was trapped in a disease-infested tent city in the middle of the desert and she had to get out. But how?

That first night, Boghos told her how. While they were lying awake waiting for sleep, Rosmerta pushed Boghos for answers. "Why are you so despondent?"

"I'm not. Leave me alone."

"Come on Boghos. We've been through too much together. Something is wrong. What is it?"

"I told you, nothing is wrong. I'm okay. Just leave me alone."

"You're not okay. Something happened between A'zaz and here. What was it?"

He sighed. "The money," he said. "I made a deal with the trailing gendarme. He took my gold coins and said he would let me slip away when we entered Aleppo. The bastard reneged. He took my money, then wouldn't let me leave the caravan."

"What about me? Was I part of this deal, or were you planning on leaving me to rot in here?"

Boghos didn't answer. A look of shock crossed his face, followed quickly by shame. He was caught out and he knew it. He hadn't even thought about Rosmerta. He was so used to being on his own that it hadn't even occurred to him that he should negotiate her release too.

Rosmerta rolled over, showing her back to the traitor. She had money too. And she knew the guards at the gates were open to bribery. She might fail, too, but it was worth a try.

Bribery

Rosmerta woke in a panic. There was a commotion at the east end of the camp, and she was alone. A scream erupted behind her. She turned to see Boghos running towards her, pushing people out of the way as he came.

"Rose, we have to go! This way." He grabbed her arm and pulled her up. They ran away from the commotion, heading deeper into the camp.

They stopped to catch their breath and watched a line of policemen encircle the small area of the camp they had just exited. "What are they doing?" Rosmerta asked.

"They're collecting the next group for deportation," Boghos told her.

"Deportation to where?"

"To Deir ez-Zur. Deeper into the desert."

Rosmerta was shocked. The rumors that Aleppo was the end of the line were not true. The trail of horrors just kept going. "Come on," she said. "Let's get out of here." She patted her right hip where she hid the small satchel with her two gold coins.

"I thought you were mad at me," said Boghos.

"I *am* mad at you. However, the deal was that if you lost *your* money—no matter how selfish the cause—*I* would still have some. Come on."

They approached the gate to find a small man with a huge dog sitting at his feet. Rosmerta grabbed Boghos by the arm. "No," she hissed. "Not yet. We'll wait for the other guard."

"What other guard? They're all the same. Let's go."

"No, we'll wait for the guard I talked with last time I came here. He was nice. He will let us out. This guy with his dog . . . I'm not comfortable with him."

Boghos huffed in frustration. He saw the disdainful look in Rosmerta's eyes and realized that he was in no position to argue. She had the coins. If Rosmerta wanted to wait for the other guard, he would have to wait with her.

When they passed by the gate a couple hours later, the same guard was still there with his dog. Maybe the guard Rosmerta wanted to deal with didn't work today. Maybe he no longer worked at the camp at all. She was feeling desperate when they passed by the gate the fifth time, and there he was— the kind man who had believed her story about Boghos being her brother and let him out. This was their best chance.

Rosmerta approached the guard with Boghos close behind her. "Excuse me, sir."

"What do you want?" he asked in a harsh, uncaring tone.

Rosmerta hesitated. This was a mistake. But it was too late now. She was committed. "We want to go to the orphanage."

"You're too old for the orphanage. They won't help you."

Rosmerta pulled the satchel from under her clothing. "No, we're not too old. They will help us." She said again flashing a coin at the guard.

His eyes lit up.

Rosmerta relaxed a bit. This might work.

The guard recovered himself. "One coin for two people? It's more than my job's worth."

"What can I get for one coin?"

"One coin, one person."

"Okay," she said, "here's one coin. Let him go."

The guard nodded. Boghos walked a few paces beyond the guard's reach so he could make a run for it if he had to. He turned back to watch the remainder of the transaction. "One coin per person, right?" Rosmerta asked the guard. "In general, yes. Having said that, there are no hard and fast rules."

She didn't like the way this was going but she had to play it out. "What is the rule for me?" she asked.

"For you? I'm not sure. I think you are definitely worth more than one gold coin."

"But all I have is one gold coin." Rosmerta could hear the desperation in her voice.

"That's not all you have," said the guard. His eyes pressed heavily down Rosmerta's neck and over her breasts, down her abdomen and stopped between her hips.

Rosmerta found the whole thing revolting. She was filthy from walking in the desert. It was almost a week ago that she had last washed. Her clothes were a mess. Her hair was a tangled jumble and she knew she must smell awful. What could this man possibly want with her?

The guard reached out and touched Rosmerta's face. His hand began the same trip his eyes had just finished.

"You pitiful bastard!" yelled Boghos as he charged. His shoulder hit the guard in the side of his ribcage, knocking him to the ground. Boghos rolled back onto his feet, and started kicking the guard as hard as he could. He stopped, looked up at Rosmerta. His mouth opened as if to say something. A red spot of blood appeared on his forehead before the crack of a pistol registered in her ears. She jumped and let out a high-pitched shriek.

Rosmerta ran towards Boghos. The shooter ran faster and knocked her out of the way. The shooter went to Boghos, saw that he was already dead and turned to help the first guard. Rosmerta hesitated for only a moment, then broke away in the confusion. She ran through the city streets as hard and as fast as she could. Her legs burned. She ran and she ran, gasping for breath. She ran until she couldn't go on.

Panting hard, she stopped and leaned against the outer wall of the orphanage. Rosmerta wasn't sure how she had gotten here. It wasn't intentional. Or at least she didn't think it was. She looked behind her. People were staring. She tried to straighten up and walk off casually. She couldn't do it. She leaned forward, resting her hand on her knees and waited for her strength to return. When she felt well enough to move on, Rosmerta stood up straight and walked to the front gate of the orphanage. The wrought iron gates were closed, and the heavy wood doors were swinging shut beyond them. The orphanage was closed for the night.

What was she supposed to do now? She made a mental note of where the camp was and walked in the opposite direction. She didn't want to end up there again. And Boghos had probably been right—as an orphan, the orphanage was just another place to be kept from going where you wanted to go and doing what you wanted to do.

Poor Boghos. He was a dependable companion. He had come so close. He worked harder than any of them to survive, only to have it end with a bullet from one of the damn guards. It wasn't fair. Then again, none of this was fair. Was it fair that hardworking families were systematically marched to death for no other reason than being Armenian? What had Rosmerta done to deserve life while everyone else had perished? Nothing. Nothing at all. But here she was, and she had to keep going. There was no point in asking why.

Boghos had saved Rosmerta's life many times. She couldn't have made it this far without him. But now he was gone. She had to figure out the next move by herself. She knew she didn't want to be an orphan, but maybe she could get a job at the orphanage instead. Then she could leave if she ever decided she didn't want to be there anymore. She decided to go back to the orphanage in the morning and ask for a job.

As she walked on in search of a place to spend tonight, Rosmerta caught a glimpse of her reflection in a puddle. Ask for a job? Looking like this? Her clothes were in decent enough shape, but they were filthy. Her hair was a tangled mess and her face was covered in dirt. She had to get cleaned up.

Rosmerta found a small fountain in a quiet, out-of-the-way part of town. A father sat on the retaining wall with his arm around his son as he played in the cool water. While it wasn't much, it was enough to entertain a child and it would be enough for Rosmerta to get clean. As she sat in the shadows at the edge of the square, she could hear the boy laughing and she could hear the deep vibrations of the man's voice. How she missed spending time with her father.

Stop, she admonished herself. She had to stop this sentimentality and focus on the task at hand. There would be plenty of time for reminiscing later.

The man stood up and lifted his son out of the fountain and they left the square hand in hand. Once she was sure no one was watching, she moved toward the fountain. She cleaned herself as best she could and found an alcove near the orphanage where she could spend the night. She slept surprisingly well and rose with the sun, feeling refreshed.

Near East Relief

The Near East Relief Orphanage was in an old church with a back yard full of tents. A tall stone wall surrounded the entire compound. Inside the main entrance, there was a large room crowded with refugees. Lines snaked their way to tables set up at the back.

A tall man carrying a clipboard approached Rosmerta. "Name," he said flatly.

"Rosmerta Bedrosian. You won't find me on your list. I don't want a handout. I'm here for a job."

"You work here? I don't recognize you."

"No, I mean I want to work here. I don't have a job yet."

"Employment. That would be Mr. Lincoln. He's not here today. You'll have to come back tomorrow."

"What does she want?" asked a plump blonde woman entering the orphanage behind Rosmerta.

"Good morning, Mrs. Lincoln. She wants a job. I told her she'll have to come back tomorrow when Mr. Lincoln is here."

"Yes, Mr. Shultz. Thank you."

Mr. Shultz stiffened, nodded, spun on his heels and walked away.

The woman turned to Rosmerta. "And your name is?"

"Rosmerta Bedrosian."

"Rosmerta," Mrs. Lincoln repeated. "What a beautiful name for such a lovely young lady. Come with me, Rosmerta." Mrs. Lincoln led her through an open courtyard, down a narrow hallway, and into a small office. There was a desk covered with papers and rows of file cabinets along the walls.

Mrs. Lincoln sat in a high-backed swivel chair behind the desk and indicated for Rosmerta to sit in the smaller chair in front of it. "What kind of work were you looking for, Miss Bedrosian?"

Rosmerta thought quickly. "I can do anything. Cooking, cleaning... I can make clothes and care for children. I can teach if needed. Oh, and I speak French," she added as an afterthought.

"French? That's very helpful. Do you speak any English?"

"No," said Rosmerta, feeling dejected.

"That's okay, we need French instructors. To think you might be able to teach English as well... it was expecting too much, but I had to ask. When can you begin?"

"Anytime," said Rosmerta eagerly.

"And where are you living?"

"I'm... ah..."

"We have accommodations here, of course. Room and board will come out of your salary. I think you'll find it convenient. Yeva needs a roommate. Come, I'll show you the way." They walked through the orphanage to a small wooden building at the back of the compound.

Mrs. Lincoln opened the door to reveal a narrow room with a cot along each wall and a small trunk at the far end. She opened the trunk and pulled out a blanket and a pillow, which she handed to Rosmerta. "The empty cot will be yours. Use the day to explore our facility and get to know where things are. You'll start work tomorrow. The kitchen is right next door. You can get something to eat there if you're hungry. You might even meet your roommate. Yeva works in the kitchen. Oh, and get yourself a change of clothes. There is a room full of donated items next to the kitchen. Help yourself to whatever you like."

Mrs. Lincoln left. Rosmerta set her bedding down and took a seat on her cot. The room was dark and smelled of smoke. It wasn't a place you wanted to spend a lot of time, but it didn't sound as if she would have much free time anyway. She went out to look for food. Just outside her room, Rosmerta saw fresh-baked loaves of bread cooling on a shelf outside the kitchen door. To her right was the main part of the orphanage through which she had just walked, and to her left was the outer wall of the compound. Rosmerta went to examine it. She found a spot where there were scuff marks on the wall. Just above the marks, the top of the wall was damaged—possibly from a tree branch resting on it. This must have been where Boghos climbed in. The tree had been cut down. She wondered how long ago that happened. Had Boghos been unable to break in? What had he been doing for food? How had he survived?

Rosmerta saw several small jasmine plants protruding out from under the wall. She plucked a few sprigs, wrapped them up so the flowers clumped together and stuck them in her hair. Then she went to find some food and clean clothes.

After a long day of exploring her new home, Rosmerta returned to her room. It was late when Yeva finally arrived. Rosmerta had fallen asleep but was startled awake when her roommate entered.

Yeva walked in carrying a lit candle.

"Oh, that's much better," said Rosmerta.

Yeva just stared at her and sat on her cot.

"Hi, I'm Rosmerta."

"Hi."

"You must be Yeva?"

"Yeah."

"How old are you?"

"Fifteen." Yeva blew out the candle and slid it under the bed.

Yeva left early every morning to make breakfast for the orphans and she didn't get back until long after dinner was served. Sometimes, Rosmerta tried to engage her in conversation, but Yeva merely grunted at what she seemed to think were appropriate intervals. Eventually, Rosmerta gave up trying to befriend her.

Rosmerta had many responsibilities. In addition to teaching French classes throughout the day, she helped the children with their calisthenics in the morning, joined them for all their meals, and made sure that everyone settled down at night.

The first night she helped to put the children to bed, a little girl was crying. "What's the matter?" Rosmerta asked as she sat on the edge of her cot.

The girl sat up and wrapped her arms around Rosmerta.

"What is your name, sweetie?"

No response. The girl was a little older than Anaguel had been, but she was much smaller. She held Rosmerta and sobbed.

"Mina," the girl in the next cot offered. "Her name is Mina."

"Mina," said Rosmerta, "what a beautiful name. Would you like to play a game?"

Mina looked up at Rosmerta and nodded. Her tears had stopped.

"Good. I'll say a word, and you say something that rhymes with it, okay?

Mina seemed to be apprehensive, but her attention was on Rosmerta.

"Okay," Rosmerta looked into Mina's eyes and pointed to her chin. "Chin," she said, then pointed to Mina's chin. "Chin," she repeated.

Mina said nothing.

"Chin," Rosmerta said again. "What rhymes with chin?"

"Sin," Mina said, almost inaudibly.

"Yes." Rosmerta pointed to her ear. "Ear," she said.

"Fear," Mina responded.

"Excellent."

Mina smiled, wrapping her arms around Rosmerta.

"That's better," said Rosmerta. "Now it's time to get some sleep. Can you do that for me?"

Mina hugged Rosmerta even tighter, burying her head in her chest.

"It's okay, dear. I'll be back in the morning, and we can have breakfast together. Would you like that?"

Mina nodded. She didn't ease her grip.

"Okay, you get some sleep now," Rosmerta insisted as she gently eased the girl on to her back and tucked her in. "Goodnight."

After that, Mina and Rosmerta were almost inseparable. The girl followed her everywhere, holding hands when they walked and clinging to Rosmerta when they were standing still. Every night, they played a game before bed. Every morning when Rosmerta entered the dorm, Mina ran up to her and gave her a big hug.

Mina came from Adana. Her trip to Aleppo had been relatively short and mostly by rail. Her father went to fight in the war. Disease had taken her mother. She ended up in the orphanage. She didn't know where her older sister was, only saying, "She didn't come to the orphanage with me."

Mina leaned into Rosmerta. "You don't smell," she said.

"I don't smell?" Rosmerta laughed. "Do I usually smell bad?"

"No, you used to smell good."

"The jasmine? The flowers I wore in my hair. That must be the smell you remember."

"I like that smell. It makes me think of you."

Rosmerta made a mental note to pick some jasmine flowers when they bloomed again.

When she returned to her room, she was surprised to find Yeva in a giddy mood. She couldn't stop smiling as she paced the room.

"What?" asked Rosmerta. "What is it? Did you meet a boy?"

"No, I'm going home."

"Home? How can that be?"

"Well, not home, but somewhere. Sister Margaret wants to see me."

Rosmerta's eyes widened. She had heard that whenever Sister Margaret wanted to see someone, it meant someone from the outside is looking for you and you may get to leave. She had never actually met the elusive nun.

"And go where?"

"Wherever the person looking for you is. I wonder who it is. I bet it's my mother. I knew she'd make it."

"When was the last time you saw her?"

"At the camp in Sivas."

"We passed through Sivas, too," said Rosmerta. *That's where I was raped the first time,* she didn't add. "What happened?"

"My mother was sick. They took her away to the hospital section. Or that's what they told us. Then they said we had to move out. I told them I couldn't go, that I had to get my mother. They wouldn't listen. They forced us to leave. But now she's recovered and she is asking for me. Isn't it great?"

Yeva's eyes were pleading as if it was up to Rosmerta to make it true. Rosmerta was searching for the right response when Yeva said, "Will you come with me?"

"Go with you? You don't even know where you're going."

"Yes, I do. Sister Margaret's office is in the back of the church."

"Of course," Rosmerta laughed at her own foolishness. "I'd like to meet this Sister Margaret."

Sister Margaret

Sister Margaret was a tall, thin woman with small delicate hands and an easy smile. Rosmerta thought Sister Margaret must have the best job in the orphanage. Every day, she got to deliver the joyous news to several people that long-lost family members had been found and that they would be reunited soon.

When the girls arrived in her office, Margaret waved to a single chair in front of her desk. "One of you must be Yeva," she said.

"I am," Yeva said as she sat in the chair. Rosmerta stood beside her.

"You are Yeva Kachian? Your father is Paren Kachian?"

"Yes."

"Where are you from?"

"Constantinople," Yeva said. "We moved to Amasia when my father lost his job."

Sister Margaret sat up straight, removed her glasses and set them on her desk. "Your father is looking for you," she said to Yeva.

"What about my mother?"

Margaret raised her glasses to her eyes and glanced down at the paperwork. "Is her name Mayranoush Kachian?"

Yeva nodded.

"Your father is looking for her as well. We haven't found her. We're also looking for a . . ." She checked her notes again, "Marta Kachian. Do you know anything about where they might be?"

"My sister," Yeva explained, her voice trembling. "I don't know where they are. I last saw them at the camp in Sivas." Her eyes filled with tears.

Margaret smiled at Yeva. "That's okay, dear. You will be with your father soon. He is in London."

Yeva was crying openly now. "But my father is dead. He was in the Turkish military. They worked everyone to death."

"Apparently not. He survived and he wants to see you. Isn't that wonderful?"

Yeva nodded. Her crying only intensified.

Rosmerta took Yeva by the hand and led her out of the office. She wasn't sure if her crying was more from the disappointment of not hearing from her mother, or the relief that her father was looking for her. Yeva recovered somewhat as they walked.

"When did you last see your father?" asked Rosmerta, trying to get Yeva to focus on the good news she had just received.

"When they recruited him into the army."

"How long ago was that?"

"Almost five years," Yeva said, starting to sound frustrated again.

"What did he do before he was in the army?"

"He was a diplomat," she said proudly. "He was in the government, working in the English embassy."

"He already speaks English. That will be helpful."

"Yes of course. He taught us, too."

"You speak English?"

"Of course," Yeva said.

"Can you teach me?"

"I guess. You'll have to learn fast."

"Teach me the basics. I can learn the finer points later."

Having something to do while she waited to go to London helped Yeva to relax during what was otherwise a nerve-racking process of paperwork, waiting, interviews, more paperwork, and even more waiting. Over the next three weeks, Rosmerta absorbed everything she could from their English lessons. Then Yeva left for her next adventure.

Rosmerta missed her friend. Yeva had been slow to warm to her, but the last few weeks had been fun. Now Rosmerta was alone again. After a few days, Mrs. Lincoln informed her that she would be relocating to another room with new roommates.

Rosmerta was relieved to learn that she only had three roommates. Some of the orphans lived in tents with forty people crowded into them. She was nervous when she entered her new room for the first time. She was immediately greeted by a short, skinny girl with long, straight black hair.

"Hi, I'm Galina Kountouriotis."

"You're Greek? How did you get here?"

"I'm from Samsun. After deportation, we made our way to Sivas, where my parents died of Typhus. The next couple months were terrible. Somehow I ended up here."

"Yeah, we came through Sivas as well." Galina seemed to be upset. Rosmerta thought she should change the subject. "Do you miss Samsun?"

"Samsun is amazing. It's on the Black Sea surrounded by green hills. Mostly, I miss the water. Of course, it's nice here too." Galina wiped her eyes and smiled. "The people here are amazing. You will like it here."

Two girls walked into the room. "Oh, and these are our other roommates, Marta and Kristina Jebejian," said Galina.

"Hello," the two girls said in unison. They skipped to one of the beds, sat down, leaned into each other so that their foreheads were almost touching and giggled.

"They're identical twins. Isn't that great? I've never known identical twins before. They don't bother much with anyone else. I guess that's just how twins are." Galina leaned in to Rosmerta and whispered, "Don't worry, I can't tell them apart either."

"What do you do here for work?"

"I work with nurse Martha. She's French. Actually, I think she's American, but her family comes from France. I'm going to live in France with my brother, Apel."

"Oh Galina, I'm so happy for you! When are you leaving?"

"I don't know. He was working in France when we were deported. It's just a matter of time before he finds me here. And I bet he'd be happy to help you too."

"That would be nice. I bet France is nicer than here." Rosmerta knew it would never happen. Like Rosmerta, Galina was alone. The two became inseparable. They talked about the families they had lost and what they hoped would happen next. Rosmerta soon learned that Galina was a high-strung person with unbounded optimism. Whenever anything went wrong, she reset the clock and insisted that from now on everything would be fine. She told everyone that after all they had suffered, the future would have to be wonderful. In fact, it seemed she was always talking. Galina irritated many people, but Rosmerta liked her. She wasn't sure how anyone could be so upbeat after enduring so much pain. Galina's enthusiasm was a nice change from the misery that she had lived with for so long.

Hope Restore

Rosmerta was confused when she and Galina returned to their room one day and the twins told them that Sister Margaret wanted to see Rosmerta. *This has to be a mistake,* she thought. Who would be looking for her?

She entered the office to find Sister Margaret sitting behind her desk with a single candle burning. Rosmerta remembered thinking that Sister Margaret had the best job in the world. Today, she couldn't help but notice how exhausted the nun was. Sister Margaret took her job very seriously and made it her personal mission to reunite as many families as possible. To achieve this, she stayed up long hours making phone calls and writing letters. The strain was beginning to show. Margaret smiled when Rosmerta entered, but her energy seemed depleted. Rosmerta noticed Margaret's reserve and took it as a bad sign.

"You called for me?"

"Yes," Margaret said, rubbing her eyes. "Please have a seat. Rosmerta, I understand you are alone here—you have no family members with you, I mean."

"Yes, sister."

"Do you have an uncle in America?

"No," replied Rosmerta. Her heart sank. She had been right all along. It had been a mistake. It was only then that Rosmerta realized how much she had gotten her hopes up. It seemed stupid now—after all, there was no one left. It was all too easy to cling to hope, any hope, even when you knew there wasn't any real hope to cling to.

"Are you sure? There's a Margos Elmassian who claims you are his niece."

Rosmerta was startled. "Uncle Margos? He's alive?"

"You do know him. I have an address for you. You can write to him and confirm that he is your uncle. He wants to bring you to America to live with his family. But let's not get ahead of ourselves. Here is the information. You should write right away. Please remember that even if this is your uncle, it will take time and money to get you to America."

Rosmerta left Sister Margaret's office in a daze. After all this time, after so much misery, Uncle Margos had found her and wanted her to go to America to live. It was all so surreal.

Galina was ecstatic when Rosmerta told her. "See?" she said. "And soon my brother will contact me and then we'll both get out of here. I told you it would all work out."

Rosmerta wrote a letter to Margos, telling him all about her travels and that she was the last of the Bedrosians. She told him about the day of the deportation, about her father being taken away with the other men never to be seen again. She told him about the endless days of trudging across Anatolia, the heat, the cold, the lice, the scabies, and the sunburn. She told him about the mountains and the desert. She told Margos about the attacks by the Special Organization but also about the kindness of Rasim Sengor. She wrote about the people who saved her life and helped her to find her way when she could no longer do it on her own. She didn't mention the rapes. Somehow, she still found that too embarrassing.

Rosmerta knew she had to tell Margos what he wanted to know most. She had to tell him that Shushawn and Boghos were dead. She also had to tell him how his brave son had fought and struggled to survive and how he had helped so many others in the face of such overwhelming odds. Without him, Rosmerta knew, she would not be alive to write this letter. But how could Rosmerta tell his father that?

She found the process of writing down her story to be somehow liberating. The world had conspired against her and thrown everything it had at her and she was still here. This was her story. She owned it now. She didn't need to share it. Not yet anyway.

She threw away her letter and started over.

Dear Uncle Margos,

It is a great joy to learn that you are well. It is my sad duty to inform you that I am the only survivor in the family. Shushawn died protecting her baby Megerdich, and Boghos was with me until a year ago. He died as he lived since you last saw him—helping others.

Yours in love and hope,
Rosmerta

It was six weeks before Rosmerta heard back from Margos. She was concerned that her blunt approach had upset him and maybe he wouldn't write back. When the letter arrived, Margos said that he was glad Boghos had been with family to the end and thanked Rosmerta for telling him what had happened. He had, of course, hoped for better news, but was glad now that at least he knew his son's fate.

The letter had instructions for Rosmerta. Margos explained how he would get money and tickets to her, what she needed to do to get the proper paperwork for travel, and everything she needed to do when she arrived in the United States.

Another five weeks passed before the money arrived. There was enough for Rosmerta to pay the fees for all the necessary documents for travel from Aleppo to Latakia, where she was to book passage on a ship to Portsmouth and then on to New York.

When the day of her departure arrived, Rosmerta was uncertain. For weeks she had planned, worried, and planned again. She had thought about her life on the march and how much better it would be in America. Of course, she also thought about her life in Bayburt. She remembered the simple joy of sitting on her father's lap and watching the sunset. She even remembered fondly how she used to sit on the ground with her second father Rasim and watch the birds fly off to their new lives.

That was it, wasn't it? Her old lives were over. There was no way back. Of course, the constant trudging through the desert and over mountains and across rushing rivers was over, too. Yes, it was time for Rosmerta to leave the nest. America was a new adventure full of its own challenges. At least it was not a camp or another march. She did still have family, and it was time to go to them.

Saying goodbye to Galina was hard, of course. Galina's endless optimism made it easier. Rosmerta wasn't convinced by her story about a brother in Paris. Did he even exist? Rosmerta wasn't sure what to believe, but she didn't see the point in pressing the matter. She hugged her friend and wished her well.

Now the really hard part, she thought. She found Mina sitting by herself, leaning against the outer wall of the orphanage near the jasmine plants.

"I like it here," Mina said.

"I like it here too," replied Rosmerta. "Mina, I have to tell you something."

"You're leaving, aren't you?" The little girl had tears in her eyes.

"Yes, I'm leaving."

"And you're not coming back?"

"No," said Rosmerta. "I'm going to live with my family in America. I won't be able to return." Rosmerta reached across Mina and grabbed a fist full of jasmine. She twisted it up, leaving a clump of flowers at one end and slid the stems into Mina's hair. "Goodbye, Mina. I will always think of you whenever I smell jasmine."

Mina pulled the flowers from her hair and brought them to her nose. She inhaled deeply. "Goodbye," she said. She sat quietly, no longer making eye contact.

Next, Rosmerta went to the office to say goodbye to Mrs. Lincoln.

Tears were running down Rosmerta's face. "How can I thank you enough?" she said. "Without the orphanage, I would still be crawling around the streets of Aleppo looking for food. You saved my life."

"Rosmerta," said Mrs. Lincoln as she pulled her into an all-encompassing embrace. "It is I who should be thanking you. You have been an excellent teacher. I don't know how we'll manage without you." She put her hands on Rosmerta's shoulders and looked deep into her eyes. "I wish you all the best, Rosmerta Bedrosian. You deserve a little peace in your life."

"Thank you, Mrs. Lincoln."

"I'm afraid I must ask you one last favor," Mrs. Lincoln said with a touch of desperation that made Rosmerta uneasy. "Sister Margaret has worked incredibly hard to get the outcome that you are fortunate enough to be experiencing. Could you please go and say goodbye to her? It would mean so much to her."

"Oh, yes, of course! I should have gone to her first. I didn't think."

"It's okay, dear. Go see her. And do enjoy your life in America. I hope you realize how lucky you are to have relatives who want you so much. It is a great gift."

When Rosmerta got to Sister Margaret's office, the nun was sitting at her desk writing a letter.

"Sister?" said Rosmerta, not sure if she should be interrupting. There was no response. "Sister," she said a bit more loudly.

"Rosmerta! What can I do for you?" Margaret smiled, but there was no joy in the expression. Rosmerta could see the strain that Margaret was under. There were black circles around her eyes and deep lines cut into her face.

"Sister, I wanted to say goodbye. I'm leaving for America. Thank you for your help. I couldn't have arranged this without you." As she said it, she realized how true it was. She hadn't even known that Uncle Margos was out there. Margaret had found his information and somehow managed to connect it to Rosmerta. She completed all the paperwork with the US embassy and organized her travel. Without Margaret, there would be no reunion in America and no place for Rosmerta to go. And the kindly nun did this for several people every day.

Margaret stood up. "My dear child," she said as she came around the desk with her arms extended. "It was my pleasure. I am delighted that we were able to create a happy ending for you. It is such a rare event. I wish you all the best in your new life."

Rosmerta knew that everything Margaret said was heartfelt. Still, she saw sadness in her eyes. She hugged Margaret as hard as she could. "Thank you," she said.

"You are very welcome." Margaret was crying now. They were happy tears. "And thank you for coming to see me. It is always a joy to see one of my success stories. Do you have your tickets?"

Rosmerta understood now why Mrs. Lincoln asked her to do this. Sister Margaret needed a win and Rosmerta was glad she could provide it. "Yes, Sister. Thanks to you, I have everything."

Rosmerta returned to the front gate and climbed into the back of a truck. Wooden side panels held her and several other travelers in the open bed with their luggage. The vehicle moved into the city. Aleppo seemed smaller now, and somehow less intimidating. The vibrant city was full of frantic activity and seemingly random motion, but was still comfortable in a familiar way. While Rosmerta was excited about her trip, she couldn't help feeling a little nostalgic. Not that Aleppo held any particular place in her heart; it was just that leaving the city meant leaving behind the last vestiges of her old life. She was leaving any hope of returning to anything she had once called home. Not that she had any illusions about returning to Bayburt—she knew there was nothing there for her. Now even the possibility was gone.

They skirted the edge of the camp, past the spot where Boghos was shot, and around the train station. The truck passed through the city and veered west towards Latakia.

They moved quickly through the countryside. The scenery was the familiar barren desert for most of the trip. All at once, as if they had been magically transported to another land, everything was green. The change in color increased Rosmerta's excitement. She was really leaving the desert behind.

Rosmerta smelled the salt air before they reached Latakia. This was her first experience of a seaside town, so the saltiness didn't hold any meaning for her except that she recognized it as being different. And different was bound to be better. She liked the smell. She took this as a good sign. She knew that many things would be different from now on.

Latakia

Good or not, change was stressful, and Rosmerta was apprehensive as she disembarked from the vehicle. She walked up to the mission door and knocked tentatively. The door creaked, and a short, dark-haired woman appeared in the sliver that opened before her.

"Hello," said Rosmerta. "You have a room waiting for me."

"Who are you?"

"Rosmerta Bedrosian. Here, I have this." She slid a letter of introduction from Mrs. Lincoln through the gap.

The woman read the letter and opened the door wider. "This way," she said.

Rosmerta followed her to a small room just off the landing at the top of a flight of stairs. The woman turned and left without a word. Rosmerta collapsed on the bed and fell asleep almost immediately.

The first light of a new day streamed through the window and brought her back to the world. It was early—too early to bang around the mission house without waking everyone else. She was restless and she wanted to get started. She walked into the city and headed for the harbor. Her boat wasn't leaving for another two days, but she wanted to know where it was docked.

Latakia was coming to life in the cool of the early morning air. The harbor was busier than the rest of the city. Fishermen start early. Several boats were already making their way past the sea wall to the fishing grounds. Bait and equipment were being loaded onto other boats that floated alongside the docks projecting out from the rocky shore. The boats were small, crewed by only a few men. There were none suitable for crossing an ocean.

Rosmerta decided she must be in the wrong place. She walked along the water's edge until she came upon another group of docks that were populated with small row boats. The next quay was even smaller. Beyond it, Rosmerta saw a long dock stretching well out into the harbor. There were no boats there, but the dock was more substantial than anything else she'd seen so far. She approached the structure and found a large building with two ticket windows side by side. Even with the building being closed and the windows dark, this looked like the right place.

Confident that she knew where to board her ship, Rosmerta returned to the mission, anxious to get back before the heat of the afternoon. The door was locked, so she had to knock. The little woman peered out. "Well?"

"It's me, madam. I am staying in the room upstairs."

"We have no more room." The door closed.

Rosmerta knocked again. A slight crack of the door and an eye appeared. "What do you want?"

"I'm Rosmerta. I spent last night here."

"What are you doing out there?" The door opened just enough for Rosmerta to squeeze through. "Get back to your room."

Rosmerta scurried upstairs and closed her door. It was hours before hunger overcame her anxiety and she slipped back out, looking for food. She was informed that breakfast was over and dinner would be served at 5:00.

Rosmerta returned to her room and waited for dinner. She would be glad to get out of this place.

When it was time to leave, the mission provided a guide to show Rosmerta to her boat. It was a good thing too, because the boat departed from the other end of the town. The areas of the harbor that Rosmerta had visited when she first arrived in Latakia were used only by a few small ferries and by local fishermen providing for their own families. The main commercial part of the harbor was much larger. There were navy vessels from England and large fishing vessels with heavy gear on deck. Rosmerta was set to sail on the HMS *Olympia*. The navy cruiser was over 300 feet long with a white hull and tan topsides that contrasted sharply with the red bottom paint. There were two tall smokestacks in the center of the ship and two even taller masts fore and aft. The *Olympia* had been converted to carry paying passengers after several years of fighting Germans on the high seas.

Olympia sailed from Syria to Portsmouth without incident. The sky was clear, and the seas were calm. Rosmerta arrived in England energized and optimistic about her future. Her mood changed shortly after departing from Portsmouth. The first day, it rained heavily. All the passengers had to remain below deck in their bunks. The slow rolling motion made Rosmerta queasy. That night, she was throwing up and couldn't sleep. After a few rough days, she was finally getting used to the motion when they sailed into a massive storm.

Rosmerta wished they could go back to the slow rhythmic rise and fall of the North Atlantic swells. Instead, the *Olympia* was being thrashed about in short choppy seas. The ship seemed to be slamming into every wave on the ocean. With each impact, the old hull groaned ominously. Several times Rosmerta was certain they had hit the wave that would break the ship in half and send them all into the water.

The *Olympia* pushed through it all and kept sailing. After a long, uncomfortable six weeks of almost constant sickness, Rosmerta was relieved to feel the seas calm and see the sun come out over the New York City skyline.

They cruised past the Statue of Liberty and slid up against the docks of lower Manhattan. There was a flurry of activity as lines were tied and ramps installed. It seemed to take forever. The mood on board the *Olympia* was nervous but hopeful. Rosmerta noticed that she was shifting her weight back and forth from one leg to the other. She stopped her motion briefly, only to find that she was doing it again soon after.

Finally, a gate was lifted on the rail of the ship. On the upper deck, Rosmerta could see people from the first- and second-class cabins streaming off the boat. She went to the stairs only to find them blocked. None of her companions from the steerage area seemed to be concerned, so Rosmerta decided it must be okay. She went back to the rail to see the last few people of class leaving the boat. Some of them slowed down enough to make sure the crew knew what a lousy job they had done, or what a crappy boat they worked on, or otherwise complain about whatever nasty thing was offending their delicate sensibilities.

The crew rolled the gangway away from the ship. Lines were released and the boat drifted away from the dock. Rosmerta's heart raced. What was happening? She was supposed to get off in New York. *Olympia* steamed to an area in the center of the harbor where other boats were moored. This is where they spent the night.

Rosmerta was too excited to get much sleep. She had traveled so far and was so close. What would happen in the morning? Would they let her in? This question had never occurred to her before. Why did it torment her now? Uncle Margos said he had everything organized, but what if he had missed something? She couldn't go back to Turkey. She knew that. In any case, it would all get resolved tomorrow.

New Beginnings

A commotion broke out as the sun rose over Manhattan. Rosmerta gathered her meager belongings and joined everyone on deck. A ferry slid beside the ship. There was another long stretch of standing around and waiting before people started transferring onto the ferry. When it was full, the ferry puttered away, leaving Rosmerta to wait again. When it returned, she pushed her way on board. The ferry skipped across the choppy water of the Hudson River and pulled up to the docks of Ellis Island. Finally, everyone was escorted off the boat and onto US soil.

Most of the passengers went to collect their checked luggage, but since Rosmerta didn't have any checked luggage, she could proceed straight into the building. She entered on the ground floor and ascended a set of stairs leading through brick arches and up to the cavernous main room of Ellis Island. The Great Hall was packed with people like herself, traveling from the Ottoman Empire, along with others from all over Europe. Rosmerta heard English, French, Dutch, German, Spanish, and Italian being spoken. There were costumes to match every accent and officials in uniform directing traffic. Rosmerta was sent to the left where she got in line and waited her turn.

The health inspector lifted Rosmerta's eyelids, checked the glands on her neck, and asked her to cough. He parted her hair with a comb and waved her through.

Rosmerta took her place at the end of another line, waiting to see a very bored looking man standing behind a tall table.

As her turn approached, Rosmerta tried to listen to the conversation. The hall was too noisy to hear anything. She watched as the man said something, then the immigrant in front of him provided an answer. The man then dutifully recorded something on his paper. After a few questions, the man nodded, and the people marched one position forward in the line.

If only she could hear what they were saying. Rosmerta was glad she had learned English from Yeva. She only wished she had had time to learn more. She knew so little. What if she couldn't understand the questions?

The process was frustratingly slow, but finally, it was Rosmerta's turn.

"Name?" the man asked without looking up.

"Rosmerta Bedrosian." She was pretty sure she got that one right.

"How do you spell that?"

"Pardon me?"

"Never mind." The man wrote something on his paper. "Age?"

"I'm sorry, my English is not so good." She was rocking back and forth nervously now.

"How old are you? How many years do you have?"

"Oh, um…I am sixteen years old."

"And where are you from?"

The more nervous she became, the harder it was to understand the questions.

"You're Armenian, correct?"

"Yes," replied Rosmerta.

"The Ottoman Empire then?"

"Yes," she answered.

"Who is your sponsor?"

"My what?"

"Who do you know in the United States?"

"Oh, my Uncle Margos Elmassian." Apparently her answer was acceptable. She thought her interrogator was ready to send her to the next station when he asked one last question. "Are you traveling alone?"

"Yes," she replied, not thinking much of it. She had been alone for a long time. Then she saw the concerned look on the questioner's face. "But I'm meeting people once I get in," she added quickly. "Remember I told you, my uncle."

The inspector held up his hand for her to stop talking. "Wait here," he said.

Rosmerta stood there in shock and panic. What had she said? She knew her grasp of English was rudimentary at best, but she thought she had done well enough. The inspector walked over to a young man at the end of the tables and pointed back at Rosmerta. She stiffened. The young man walked off and the inspector returned. "It will be just a minute," he said.

Rosmerta was still shifting her weight back and forth. She had to break this habit. There was a scream from a young boy a couple tables over. Rosmerta scanned up and down the line of tables. When she first entered the Great Hall, it seemed to be one swarming mass of disorganized people. Slowly it started to make sense and she was able to discern a great deal of order and almost rigid organization that was very impressive. Suddenly it all looked like chaos again. There seemed to be arguments going on at every table. No one was getting in. There was an excuse to keep out everyone. She was going to be sent back.

A man approached Rosmerta's inspector, snapping her attention back to her own situation. The two men whispered, occasionally glancing over at her. The new man was reviewing her papers. Rosmerta wanted to scream, *"What? What are you talking about? What's going on?"* She didn't dare say anything. She stood there and awaited their final judgment.

Finally, the new man folded up Rosmerta's papers and nodded to the inspector. He approached Rosmerta and spoke in perfect Armenian. "Hello Rosmerta, my name is Vahan Kezerian. I will escort you from here to meet your family. Do you have twenty dollars?"

The relief she felt from hearing her native tongue vanished. Twenty dollars? She wasn't paying this man twenty dollars to escort her.

Vahan saw her reaction and laughed. "No, no," he said, "you need to show the guards that you have at least twenty dollars before they will let you in. It's the only thing you have left to do and then I'll help you find your uncle. I am with a group that helps Armenians get resettled in America. Women aren't allowed to leave Ellis Island unescorted. I'll go with you and help you to get headed in the right direction. You don't have to pay me."

By this point, Rosmerta was really panicked. Uncle Margos had written her about the requirement to show twenty dollars to the immigration officials before they would let you into the country. He had sent her the money. Where had she put it? She rummaged through her small sack of possessions. It wasn't there. She checked her pockets. She was about to remove her shoes to see if she had hidden the money there, when the fog in her head cleared. Excited, but still uncertain, she untied a small satchel from her belt. She opened it and exposed the money.

"Twenty dollars," Vahan confirmed. "We're ready to go."

After leaving the Ellis Island facility, they took a ferry across the river to Manhattan. From there they traveled uptown to Grand Central Station. Vahan helped Rosmerta buy a ticket, put her on a train to Worcester, Massachusetts, and said goodbye.

The train pulled into the station—a beautiful new gray granite structure with enormous American flags flying proudly from two soaring towers at the front. Union Station was a grand building among the immense brick factories and multi-story wooden homes of Worcester, Massachusetts.

Rosmerta stepped onto the platform feeling apprehensive. Would she recognize Uncle Margos?

A short man with a gray head of hair and dark mustache approached her. "Rosmerta, welcome to Worcester."

She scrutinized the man. It had been three years and so much had changed. She was a woman now, no longer the child she had been when she last saw Margos on the day he left

Bayburt. In spite of the hardship she had suffered, she had grown over a foot. Uncle Margos looked small and frail.

"Uncle Margos?" she said doubtfully. Then she saw the pendant on the man's lapel. It was the arevakhach—the Armenian symbol of eternity. "Uncle Margos!"

"Yes," he said gleefully. "I hope you're hungry. Margaret is home with the girls preparing a feast to celebrate your arrival. There will be a huge celebration with many of our new friends. Everyone is anxious for news from the mother country." He paused. "You look confused, Rosmerta. What's wrong?"

"Nothing... it's just... I've changed so much since Bayburt. How did you recognize me?"

"It hasn't been that long," laughed Margos as he pulled his long-lost niece into a bear hug. "Besides, you look so much like your mother."

Author's Notes

The characters in this story are fictional, but everything that happens to Rosmerta and her family in this story happened to many people in real life. I relocated some historical events to Bayburt, since that is where my characters started their journey. There was not one, but three deportations from Bayburt. As far as I know, no one followed Rosmerta's exact path to Massachusetts. However, to this day, there is a thriving Armenian community in Worcester.

What happened to the Armenians in the last days of the Ottoman Empire is generally referred to as the first genocide of the Twentieth Century. Regrettably, it was not the first genocide. Worse, it was not the last. On multiple occasions, Hitler referenced the atrocities committed against the Armenians as an example of what should be done to his enemies and pointed out that there were few negative consequences for those who were responsible.

The point? Failure to remember the Armenian Genocide for what it was made it difficult for the world to recognize what was happening in Germany during World War II.

To this day, the government of Turkey refuses to acknowledge the crimes committed against the Armenians between 1913 and 1923. In January 2017, Turkish parliament member Garo Paylan stated that the Armenians, Assyrians, Greeks, and Jews were "exiled from these lands or subjected to tortures as a result of large massacres and genocide." For his comments, Paylan was suspended from parliament. In July that same year, the term "Armenian Genocide" was banned within the Turkish legislature.

Shamefully, because Turkey is recognized as a valuable ally, the United States has not officially recognized the fact of the Armenian Genocide, although most states have.

As the Holocaust has taught us, failure to remember dooms us to repeat:

Genocide since World War I

Location	Ended	Aggressor	Victim	Estimate of Dead	
				Low	High
Europe	1945	Nazi Germany	Jews	6,000,000	
East Pakistan	1971	Pakistan	Bangladeshi	300,000	3,000,000
Cambodia	1979	Khmer Rouge	Cambodians	1,500,000	3,000,000
East Timor	1999	Indonesia	East Timorese	84,000	183,000
Guatemala	1983	Guatemala	Mayans	140,000	200,000
Iraq	1989	Iraq	Kurds	50,000	200,000
Bosnia	1995	Christian Serbs	Muslims	8,000	40,000
Rwanda	1994	Hutu	Tutsi	500,000	1,000,000
DRC	2004	Rebel Forces	Pygmies	60,000	70,000
Darfur	Ongoing	Sudan	'non-Arab' Darfuri	80,000	500,000
Myanmar	Ongoing	Buddhists	Muslims	1,000	3,000

I want to stress that this novel is not meant to be an indictment of Muslims. In the story, Dr. Tarik and Muhammad Kasaba were Muslims. In fact, every account I have read or heard about Armenians surviving the deportations involves their getting help from someone. In many cases, that help came from Muslims. While it is true that it was Muslims who perpetrated the atrocities against the Armenians, it was Christians who committed the Holocaust, as well as the horrors in Bosnia and Rwanda.

The sad truth is that it is part of the human condition: we are very good at categorizing each other into groups, labeling those groups, and assigning blame to them. Once we have identified a group of people as being responsible for all the ills that befall us, it is all too easy to hate them. And it is an easy path from hating a group of people to killing them. The path sometimes leads to disgusting extremes. In the case of the Democratic Republic of Congo (DRC), pygmies were hunted for food.

Especially now, when lethal means are so readily available to everyone, it is critical that we are aware of these tendencies, and that we are on the lookout for those who might act upon them. For, if we do not guard against it, it will happen again.

Thank You

Thank you for reading *Annihilation: A Story of the Armenian Genocide.* If you enjoyed it, I would be extremely grateful if you would leave a review at your favorite retailer. It is very helpful to authors to have your assistance in getting the word out about our work. If you would like more information, please visit me at www.michaelbosland.com.

Michael Bosland

Made in the USA
Middletown, DE
26 April 2021